THE
APPEARANCE
of a HERO

THE
APPEARANCE
of a HERO

The Tom Mahoney Stories

Peter Levine

ST. MARTIN'S PRESS
NEW YORK

THE APPEARANCE OF A HERO. Copyright © 2012 by Peter Levine. All rights reserved. Printed in the United States of America. For information, address St. Martin's Press, 175 Fifth Avenue, New York, N.Y. 10010.

www.stmartins.com

"How Does Your Garden Grow?" originally published in *The Missouri Review*, Volume 31, Number 3, Fall 2008; "Code Pink" originally published in *Commentary*, November 2010; "Cotillion" originally published in *The Cincinnati Review*, Volume 8.1, Winter 2010; "Havasu" originally published in *Slice Magazine*, Issue 6, Spring/Summer 2010; "La Jolla" originally published in *The Southern Review*, Volume 46, Number 2, Spring 2010; "Princess" originally published as "Booth One" in *The Southern Review*, Volume 47.3, Summer 2011; "He Tells His Father" originally published in *The Hopkins Review*, Volume 5, Number 3, Summer 2012.

ISBN 978-1-250-00122-1 (hardcover)
ISBN 978-1-250-00833-6 (e-book)

First Edition: August 2012

10 9 8 7 6 5 4 3 2 1

CONTENTS

One must have heroes, which is to say, one must create them. And they become real through our envy, our devotion. It is we who give them their majesty, their power, which we ourselves could never possess. And in turn, they give some back. But they are mortal, these heroes, just as we are. They do not last forever. They fade. They vanish. They are surpassed, forgotten—One hears of them no more.

—JAMES SALTER, *A Sport and a Pastime*

THE
APPEARANCE
of a HERO

HOW DOES YOUR GARDEN GROW?

He TELLS ME he felt it once—love. Lust, mainly, though he had hoped it would turn into love. He—a friend I know from work—is dedicated, driven, will be as good a salesman as there is (they taught us at a seminar in Dallas to learn one story and to tell that story well, tell it to any potential client: the birth of your kid, the day you won the big game, your most recent vacation—it doesn't matter what story; its only use is to begin a conversation, which will lead to a sale)—he is quick, incisive and, we all tell him, a wonderful listener.

In his personal life, however, I believe my friend is laid-back, fun to be around, attractive in all ways. I don't know him too well, but I admire him. Something about his easy way.

His lover, this woman, almost ruined him. He holds his glass of scotch and soda up to his lips and says he couldn't believe it—it was, in his life, the first time he knew he was feeling stress. Anxiety. He had been studying for the Series 7. He said he'd wake up at night in a panic. What with all that was going on with her and the test.

My friend has a chest like you wouldn't believe—thick and strong, like a swimmer's. Thick black hair.

The woman was his boss from his first job out of school. She was tan, fit, had short blond-brown hair—the type of woman who looked like she might have been a tennis instructor, or a high-impact aerobics instructor. She liked it in the ass, he tells me. That was one thing that turned him on about her. It was her favorite way, actually. It was also when he knew there was something different, and possibly wrong with her, and part of what made him fall for her so badly.

How it started, he does not tell me. Not this night, the canopy of the lounge we're at pulled back, the sky blue and void of clouds, the two of us just having drinks, a quiet place near Lake Michigan; no pressure, just two guys having cocktails: slacks and shirts and gleaming black shoes and thin belts and thin bodies. A moment without a past or a future. Well, a bit of a past—a story. His story.

This woman. Maybe they met for drinks after work, had a few (he more than she), took a few bumps of coke (he does it, but only when it's around him), had a cigarette, and then the sex. He said her body was clean and unblemished, tight; her pussy was waxed— beautiful, he tells me, *just beautiful*. There was also the issue of her being his boss. It excited him, he says. A thrill.

He is the type of man who lives for such things: the big sale, a rush. Four black coffees in the morning for my friend, and four scotch and sodas at night.

He kept his apartment and she hers. People at work knew—it wasn't a big secret. The guys at the office (it was in Arizona, he says) thought it was cool. They thought she would have been wild in bed. Was she? How was it with her? Good?

He never really told them. He never told them that once they did it in her office, during work hours—well, toward the end of the day, but still. He never told them that there was a pathos to how she liked to do it, what she liked to say—it was beyond him to think of it in terms of demeaning her—that wasn't it at all. She would say, *Fuck me in the ass. Fuck my asshole.* He had never heard such things, and he had heard a lot.

He did it.

"How did it feel?" I ask.

He takes my finger and makes a fist around it.

The other things they did together were what normal couples did. She liked to hike (he less so, but he was more than willing to do it for her). He had a hard time keeping up with her. So much energy. Over rocks, across fields, on the hard-packed desert floor, the heat bearing down on them like a mantle, they hiked to elevation. She loved to sweat. She drank hardly any water when she did these things. Her body browned. In the evenings, they would do dinner. Candles, low lights, white tablecloths, fish or salad to eat for her, beef if they had it for him, scotch and soda, cigarettes, sunburned legs touching each other under the table, sandals fallen off or dangling— the whole of the desert watching her, as if it knew she was worthy of being understood, reckoned with.

He never had to say a thing, he said. She did all the talking. But it wasn't annoying. He liked her voice. A smooth, even voice. Happiest person he'd ever met. Sunny. Really, a delight to be around. Skin tight around her mouth. Talked about the work they were doing, the money they were then making, her house, her garden that she loved—all the succulents she kept, the deck she'd built, the desert and then the mountains beyond. It was a nice home (he had seen it a few times), but it had been so sparsely decorated. She had moved in seven months ago and still there were boxes around.

She announced that she wanted to buy a pet. To share. How did that sound? Would he go in on one with her? It meant something, he felt. Sure, he said. They were moving their relationship forward. What a fantastic woman. Drank deeply from life, she did.

What he asked her that night, which was not much (she had already offered so much), was about her growing up, her childhood. She said he knew all that already. She was from Portland.

He said he knew, but he just thought it would be nice to talk about; he felt like he hadn't been the best conversationalist. As he was saying it, he realized that he had seen no pictures of her family at her place. He assumed her parents were still alive, working or retired. He knew that she was an only child. He had assumed they'd have talked about these things.

She said it had been nice, fine—very good, actually; her spirits seemed to dip and then lift as she told it, and he knew here, he tells me, that she was fabricating an upbringing that she felt would be one not that he would want to hear, but one that would be suitable to be heard.

She did not go on at length about her parents, only told him what they did (her father was a mechanical engineer and her mother was a lawyer). She then went on to tell him all about what she'd done in school, all the activities she'd been involved in, the clubs (president of the distinguished lecture series, writer for the business section of the university newspaper, intern for the dean of the school of arts and sciences), the partying she'd done there, then work: one company, where she'd worked as a personal financial adviser and then this most recent company, and then working her way up the ladder. There was no discussion of the difficulties in being a woman in a man's business, no discussion of harassment. She was happy on all subjects.

At his apartment, after work, he studying from the kind of book you'd keep a door open with. She wanted to go out, but he said he really had to study. The fan going. A clean-line apartment building. The walls were white. He had put up a number of large photographs of him and his father: playing golf, at the Cubs game—they were so close. His mother had taken them. The girlfriend never asked him about this. He had hoped that she would.

She watched television, sitting beside him. Her policy was to work hard and leave work at work. He, on the other hand, was still junior, and had to pass the exam if he wanted to move up. She told him not to worry about it. He said he was a little worried.

He had made it through college with little effort—he'd never been going for honors. He had gotten hired on charm alone. Could talk to anyone and everyone admired him. She said the exam wasn't that hard. She'd passed on her first try; she was sure he would. They'd go out and celebrate; she had a surprise for him. He asked her what. She said he'll have to wait to find out. He tells me that he couldn't wait; he desired her. She had this effect on him, got him hard right away, like a piece of lead pipe, like a truncheon, she in a T-shirt advertising a sports store and baby blue terry-cloth shorts, straddled him on the leather sofa.

Air-conditioning was coming down from the vents. The night was purple above the skylights. He says it was always like being with a goddess—and he is not a man to speak in hyperbole. He means it.

All clothes, off. Her knees on the sofa, she told (not asked, told) him to put it in her ass. He said he wanted to do it the regular way. She reached behind her. The book fell off the sofa. No, she said. My way. This way. She grabbed him, licked her other hand, wet her asshole, wet the bulb of his cock, and put him inside.

If that was how she wanted it, he tells me, then that was how. I loved her.

On the way to the pet store. They were going to get a lizard. You have never seen someone so excited, he says. She was freaking out. It was like picking up a new car. The truth was, though, I was kind of excited, too, he says. For her. But also for us. We were going to do this thing together. It would bind us. We would have to care for it together. Feed it. Talk to it. Clean the aquarium. Even though we had decided to keep it at my place. Though her place was so much larger, so much more light (she even had a good spot for it in the great room). She promised she would always be over to help.

At the store, they looked around at the lizards. They had snakes, too. But snakes you had to feed mice, and it was too big a hassle. There were salamanders—too small.

Then they saw it—this iguana—not moving, really, just sitting in its glass aquarium, its lids folding upward. Skinny green thing. It had this look on its face, he says. He didn't see how someone could be so excited by an iguana. It didn't really *do* anything. The pet store smelled like dog food and piss. He didn't like it very much. In fact, he was a pretty clean guy. He liked the toothpaste tube to be clean, for instance. That was one thing she was never good at—always left crap around the toothpaste.

She declared the iguana would be named Hector. She asked him, squeezing him on his ass, if he liked that name. He didn't really, but he said he did. She didn't mean it in the Greek way. But he decided

he was at least going to think of it like that. He wanted to get out of
the pet store. The lights were too bright and unnatural; he wanted
to get back into the dry heat of the desert, drive with the top down,
the good feeling of the hot leather against your back. She was talking fast to the store clerk, a young Hispanic guy, who was a bit
startled by her energy. My friend shared a look with him. The look
also said that it'd be worth it—to be with her.

They left: Hector the Iguana, a giant glass aquarium, a plastic
bag full of iguana food and vitamin supplements, aquarium
accoutrements—including a fake log. They put all this in the trunk.
But not Hector. Hector sat on her lap. She stroked him. He looked
nervous. My friend tells me he's pretty sure the animal was nervous.
She was very aggressive about stroking it. He wanted to talk to her
about the feeding schedule. Stucco and adobe-colored strip malls
were going past. The mountains, in the distance, and all the land—
which threatened to assume the city, to run them out. She said she'd
take great care of him. They say that iguanas form serious emo-
tional attachments to people, he reminded her.

When they got back to his place, she watched as he put the aquarium together, put the water attachment on, filled it, took Hector
from her. She resisted, said she wanted to hold him longer; he said
the clerk had told them Hector needed to get adjusted to his aquarium.
He grabbed the lizard: hot and expanding in his hands—knowing it
immediately preferred him, could feel it falling in love with him,
could feel it wanting to be a buddy with him, and *he* then resisted it,
put it in the aquarium, dropping it on the soft wood chips. Here you
go, buddy.

Such a pathetic creature, he says. I had hoped the name would give
it some honor, but still, it looked a little sad. I knew then, he tells me,
that I was going to have to give more of myself to it than I had planned,
and I know this about my friend: There is only so much to give.

She came over to look at it. Her smell, he tells me, was out of this
world. Like she was always walking out of the shower. It's crazy,

what with all this woman had done. She once told him that she sodomized a guy with a carrot. She said that she would do the same thing for him if he wanted. He didn't want that. She touched him, staring at Hector. It was a sunny day, and he said it was too bad he had to study. He went over to the couch.

But of course, he says, asking the bartender for another scotch and soda, he didn't do that. He didn't study. He desperately needed to. There was more to learn. He had a life to think about. He wanted it to be old-fashioned. Where he could support the family all on his own. It was silly, he admits, but it was what he wanted. This test seemed to him to be the first barrier to beginning it—how odd, he tells me, that up until that point, life had seemed like a smooth plane, unobstructed.

She asked him if he'd fuck her up against the window of his apartment. He said, No, not right now. He almost couldn't believe that she would just say it like that—even though she had said this sort of thing many times. I've got to study. Do this first, she said. She wriggled out of her khaki shorts—always wriggling out of her shorts, he says. She leaned over the windowsill. She started playing with her pussy and then her asshole. She said she wanted Hector to watch his parents do it. He said that was gross, but what the hell could he do about it?

He did it. As he did it, he thought to himself that he was surely in love—this was what love was. He liked to see the desert outside. It was flat and clean and dry. Everything was in its place. It was so quiet. All one could hear was the air-conditioning. And her moaning. His cock in her ass.

At times, he tells me, he could feel her ass contracting, and maybe, once, he says, in all the times they did it that way, her having to shit. Could feel it pushing up against him. He didn't care, or care whatever his cock might have looked like afterward. The extremity of the act must have equaled, or been commensurate with, the extremity of emotion. That emotion being love. His first real one.

That lizard, he says. I learned something about life from that lizard.

He had to go to a conference for a week or so back here in Chicago. Visited his parents, who still lived here. Stayed downtown at the old Hotel Nikko. It was good, because he needed the evenings in his room to study. She had a key to his place, was practically living there anyhow, taking care of Hector. At the conference, they were talking about growth equities, capital opportunities, focus funds. The stuff was interesting to him. He made friends so easily. They went out to lunch, all these guys. The House of Blues. Talked about midwestern college sports. They listened as my friend talked—he had been an athlete in college. They talked about making a lot of money.

But he was calling this girl during his breaks, and she wasn't answering the fucking phone, he says. He couldn't figure out where she was. He called her at work and the secretary said that she'd called in sick. So he called her house, his apartment. Some colleagues he spoke to (he said it was a work-related matter)—they didn't know any more than the secretary. He missed a call from her—she just said, Hey, it's me. She did not tell him not to be worried, that she was okay—none of this she mentioned. He'd left a dozen or so messages for her and all she had for him is *Hey, it's me*? Like nothing was going on.

At night, in this hotel room. He was leaving the following day. He was calling her constantly. This was so unlike him. He felt like something essential had been excised from him and only now did he realize how vital it was to his existence.

He thought about something that never happened, but which he sort of *wished* had happened. An evening at her home. Her wide bed. She naked in the bed. Had sex before, but now they're sleeping. She is, at least. But not him. He's up. He's naked and he leaves her bed and opens the sliding patio door and walks onto a small balcony. The backyard is the desert, blue and unmoving.

The Saguaro sleeping, the coyotes sleeping, the desert mice, the cracks in the earth taking in air and no water—he can hear the rivers under the layer of dry earth swimming, rumbling like a conveyor belt under the desert crust. And he, my friend, watching all this, and feeling completely light, completely unrestricted. The feeling you have after you come, after you shit, after you swim. All manner of blue is covering the desert on this night he's imagining. Pores are shrinking on his kind face. His chest is widening. Blood is filling the veins in his arms from the lovemaking. And he realizes that this is what peace is. This is all right, he thinks.

It was all a fiction, though. He had his phone on his chest, waiting for her to call. He was trying to study. He fell asleep.

At one point, he had a dream that his phone *was* going—that it was her. She'd been in an accident. Had to go up to Portland to see her folks (her mother had fallen and broken her hip and the father needed her help), but she couldn't fly—there was bad weather up there—so she'd decided to drive. Another car on the highway. Rain. The accident was bad. She'd be okay. She was only now just coming out of the surgery—she had a bad gash on her leg and a dislocated shoulder and they'd doped her up—and he was the first one after her parents that she'd called. She'd be okay. She'd be back to normal soon. Could he come to see her? She needed him. In the dream, he told her he was already on his way.

But it wasn't the phone and it wasn't anything. He felt, prayed, that the dream was real. But he had an empty-stomach feeling, knowing that it wasn't. He was sweating and his heart was slowing down. He thought that he was dying. He was pretty sure he was having a heart attack, wondered if somehow, someone would find her and tell her that he had died, for he would want her to be at his funeral—even with his parents—to show them what a great girl he had found, what she might have been like as a daughter-in-law. His parents had wanted him to return to Chicago immediately after college, but he hadn't, and he thought she would be evidence of a life that he had made for himself out west.

But this pain. It was cool in the room, but he was roasting, and went into the bathroom (too bright) and got sick all over the place. Had to bend over and clean up all the filth with toilet paper. He went back to his bed, back under the covers, felt worse than he'd ever felt in his life. His life had been too easy; it had not prepared him for this.

He arrived home late afternoon, went directly back to his apartment. No messages from her. He called in to his office and the secretary, who knew that he'd been sleeping with the boss, said with irritation that she was still not in. In fact, they didn't know where she was. But she was the head of the little retail office, so if she wanted to take off, she could. He said okay. He went to check on Hector. The animal was all white, like cigarette ash. This is what happens when iguanas don't get enough light, the proper nutrition. She hadn't watered it, either—probably the entire week. It had a look on its face like it wanted to die. He felt sympathy toward it. The shades were drawn in his cool apartment. She was supposed to come and open them and feed Hector. But of course, none of that. He took it out of the cage. It felt lighter, of course. The texture of its skin as if it were melting.

And then my friend, a happy man, jovial—he tells me that he cried. He never wanted it. He can't remember the last time he'd cried.

He opened up the shade. Its claws on his shirt felt so odd. He took its little water feeder and put it to Hector's mouth. The pathetic thing—it opened its mouth to receive. He stood by the window. The girlfriend, his lover, she might have been dead. It was possible.

But he knew that this was not the case. He knew that her disappearance was an eventuality. He'd known, that first time, something was wrong about her. Too happy, too greedy with the love. And being a guy—he couldn't think straight. A woman who liked it in the ass? A woman who wanted to fuck all the time? How could he have thought properly about things? One can't expect such things from a mortal, he tells me.

He held the iguana the way one would hold a baby.

He tells me it really would have been great if she could have met his family, or if he could have introduced her to them. He'd had girlfriends before, sure, but none so outgoing and nice. The kind you really think about spending holidays with, the kind you'd want your kids to be around because she's so fun and would make them laugh all the time and do fun stuff with. In truth, he tells me, he sort of imagined a whole life with her. A good one, too. One of those outdoor-activity kind of families. Maybe a son and a daughter who did sports. A desert life, all new.

Hikes through orange canyons with a flake of blue sky above, following dried-out riverbeds, backpacks and hiking boots and bottled water and a compass and knife and floppy hats; the smell on all of them of sunblock, streaks of white on noses and cheeks. Sitting with his family—he watching them and feeling, what? Pride, certainly, but also serenity, a life fully realized, and the wonderment of how one could go so long and not know that one had been living a half-life. She was the other half. It was something about the desert, and this woman, he says.

He was still so young—there was no reason, other than she was older than he was, just a handful of years, that it might not have happened.

That week, he did the regular stuff. He was broken and was beginning to heal. You get over love, don't you? A broken heart. At work on Monday, they said that she—his woman—had taken a leave of absence. Some of the guys asked him what was up and he said that he didn't know. He had his test at the end of the week.

He tried to get her out of his mind. He went to work, worked hard. Drank a lot of coffee. He stopped trying to get ahold of her. There was no playbook for what to do when a lover goes missing, one whom you are not committed to necessarily, or rather, only committed to through a pet. That was the whole of their estate. He ran in the evenings, in the heat. Came home, took care of Hector. It licked the sweat off him, off the backs of his hands. Its tongue was like a little soft spike. He held it for a bit, because he knew that iguanas were especially clingy. Dumb thing, he thought. God, he thought. The desert. The woman, the heat.

He showered, studied. Had a drink and then another. Scotch and soda. His heart was bruised. Maybe had a joint. To get by. Maybe other stuff.

The week went. Hector was turning green again and fattening.

He came home from work Friday night, the day before the exam, and there she was. She looked tired—like something had emptied out from her.

"Hey," she said.

"Where were you?"

"Oh. I had to take off for a bit. I had some things I had to take care of."

He was wholly unprepared. The love he felt went back into his heart. It could be the three of them again. The lizard, too. Why not the lizard? She was safe. He went to hug her. She hugged him a little, but there was nothing there—no recollection of what they had been doing, or had done, or of a future they might have had.

"Where did you go?"

"Los Angeles."

"I thought you were dead."

"Nope," she said. "Still alive." She was gathering certain things. She had with her a tote bag. She was in the bathroom.

"I just—I tried calling you. My God. At work, they didn't know where you were, either."

"I don't work there anymore," she said.

"What?"

"I quit. I needed a change," she said casually.

He was not understanding this. Nor should he. In his life, he had never encountered someone like her and so he did not recognize the pattern: the highs and the lows—didn't know what that signaled, didn't know that a person could behave this way. He had something so good. It was a kind of passion, which he misunderstood to be love. He didn't know such things were transient, that she would never be a dear woman.

"You just left. Do you think that's fair? I was worried half to death. It was killing me. I thought I'd had a heart attack."

"Well, look. We're not married," she said.

"Hector. You left him alone while I was gone. The dumb fucking lizard. I didn't even want it. It almost died, you know."

"You loved it," she said. And here she lifted the lid of the cage, reached into it, and pulled it out. She was looking at it like something foreign and disgusting. It tried to scramble out of her hands, to move toward him—he was the one the creature loved. She grabbed it by the tail, and sure enough, he tells me, the fucking tail came off. It detached.

"Can that happen?" I ask.

"Yeah," he says. "And it doesn't grow back." Hector went under the table. For a second, she had a remorseful look, but that was it. She was holding the tail. She laid the tail on the coffee table. She went back into the bathroom and continued to collect her things: toothbrush, makeup, floss—all things that were hers. These resources he'd never thought about. That which aided in her mystique.

He just stood in his little living room. It was all so unbelievable to him. The desert was white and yellow. Suddenly, he felt very old.

He leaned down and there was the tail. What the fuck? he thought. He scooped up Hector from under the table. In his hands, it lowered its head. Never was it a large creature. It had little flat circles for ears. An ugly animal.

"Okay," she said, glumly.

"I don't understand this. I don't get any of this," he said, the lizard in his hand.

"Well, you're still young. But this happens."

She didn't apologize for nearly killing him, with the whole panic attack business (he didn't know it was that), the lizard, for killing his young heart, for killing his belief in certain things:

order, love, sex—the belief that they could all be magnified, all be extreme and still work.

He didn't get it, he tells me, because there was nothing to get. The thing was, he explains, this fucking girl—this beautiful, fucked-up girl—was crazy. But not crazy in the way all girls are crazy, but literally. Later, she wrote him from Oregon. She said she was sorry about Hector. She told him that she was sorry for the whole mess of things and that she was only just now waking up.

"What about Hector?" I ask.

"I let him go," he says. Let the green thing out into the desert. "I didn't fucking want it."

As for the test, he passed it. He took it and passed it and that was it. He got laid off from the job he was in anyhow. A lot of people did around that time. I was one, too.

He got a good severance package and finally returned home, where he met me, where I myself was working a new job and attempting to reorganize that which I had found disorganized in a previous life, one far less interesting than his.

He's finished his drinks and I mine, and the night is black and terrific. He wants to know if I want to go out with him. More drinks. Maybe meet some women. I'm surprised he still has the spirit for that, though he *is* young and it was some time ago now—that business with the old girlfriend.

No, I tell him. I'm beat. I'm done for. He takes out his billfold and I tell him that I've got it this time and he protests, frowning, and says no, and I say that I insist, putting my hand over his as he reaches for the check.

"So, Robbie. That's the story. I hope it was one you wanted to hear," he says.

"Well, it was pretty funny," I say, though I'm not sure it is funny. Mostly, I find it sad, and sad in a way I cannot name. And as I leave, he and I parting ways, me walking back to my car, and to a form of an evening much different, I am sure, than the one he will enjoy, I think that the sadness is the sadness you feel when you see someone innocent, like a child, get bullied. You want to protect the victim. You want them to be ignorant of the pain.

Parked near the lake is my car—a beautiful silver thing on which I blew my entire bonus, and which, I feel, was entirely worth it.

That conference—the one we had in Dallas—where they said you only need to know one story. Well, this is my story. His story. You're lucky if you enjoy even a fraction of what he enjoyed—the pleasure, the ecstasy—while avoiding the pain. You simply can't have it all. There *are* still great pleasures in the world. But you have to enjoy them sparingly. Any decent American could tell you that. Even in this station in my life, I know it.

HAVASU

LATE FRIDAY AFTERNOON. Tom stands in the office doorway, his white shirt unwrinkled, his blue tie neat and sharp. His face still full of color, though it's February and it seems as if the city hasn't seen sunlight since October.

"Are you getting out of here soon?" Tom asks. He's ready to leave. There's a happy hour in Wrigleyville. "We can go together."

"I don't know," Cody says. "No. Probably not. Hey, are you going to that meeting on Monday morning? The one at seven with the lawyers?"

"You're going to *that*?" Tom says, raising his hand up to his forehead. "Oh, no. Oh, that's just—Jesus. Come out with us tonight. You gotta get out of here."

Cody admires this about Tom. A man who can drink himself through winter. Outside, it's snowing, and as far up as they are, Michigan Avenue looks surreal, the cars' lights on Wacker Drive softened through the snow, the lights of the Tribune building dull blue and otherworldly.

"I know. Jesus, do I," Cody says. "I'm just too beat. I can't."

Cody had followed Tom to Chicago. Tom had had a rough go of it with a woman he'd been seeing in Arizona after school, and his father had gotten him a job at a friend's firm. Tom had told Cody there was an opening if he wanted it. At the very least, they could make some money. Cody had little keeping him at home.

"We gotta fix you up," says Tom. He is smiling. Something has come to him. "Listen, you're getting a massage. I have this girl. I'm calling to make you an appointment for tomorrow. I'll tell them it's your birthday. What time?"

"What? No. I mean, thanks, but no."

Tom raises his hand. Once a terrific left fielder.

"I'm doing this for you. Good mentoring, let's say. Just tell me what time. That's all I need to know."

Cody is hesitant. He knows what Tom is into. He was once, too, but that part seems an aspect of a former life. Moreover, he's never had a massage from someone who wasn't a trainer, and is embarrassed to admit it.

"Three?"

"Done and done," Tom says, walking away.

"Listen! Tom—" Cody shouts, "I don't want—"

"Be there at three. And meet us out later!" he says from down the hall.

That evening, Tom calls him, though Cody lets it go to voice mail. He's watching Game 7 of the 1988 National League Championships on ESPN Classic. Orel Hershiser. Jesus Christ. An arm that wouldn't quit. A sportswriter had once written the same thing about Cody. Which was true.

The message, choppy over the sound of the bar, is Tom, drunk, shouting: "Daniels! Where are you? Hey, man, listen. There's this girl here, Dana—I think she'd be great for you. I just—you two might—I don't know. I mentioned you to her. Come meet us. I can't—yeah, so come meet us."

Cody can hear a girl's voice in the background. She's saying to someone, not Tom, *"We'll meet them later. Later! What? Who?"*

Tom adds, "Oh, and you're on for three o'clock tomorrow. Thank me Monday."

It's not a massage parlor, nor is it a spa. It's just the bottom floor of a three-story brownstone on a residential street. The waiting room is

decorated to look like a spa, though it's a little funny. There are vo-
tives in long, arching glass holders, a black stand-alone fountain one
would buy on sale at a hardware store, a small teapot with Styro-
foam cups and packets of sweetener beside it.

Cody walks over to an opening in the wall that seems to serve as
a counter, where a man—he resembles the sports commentator Jim
Rome—sits reading a magazine: *World Affairs*. Cody tells him his
name and that he's here for a three o'clock appointment.

"Okay," he says, looking over at a thick black appointment book.
He sounds as if he's from Eastern Europe. "You are Cody?"

"Yes."

"Have a seat, please. Helen will be out with you in a moment."

Cody stands there for a second. He thinks the man said Helen,
but he might have said Ellen or Elena—Cody is not sure. He's nervous. Part of it is his body, which is so thin, the thinnest it's ever
been. The man returns to reading his magazine and Cody goes to
sit in a small wicker chair.

Trying to relax, he tells himself that there is very little this woman
can do or say or offer that he hasn't already enjoyed, or been a par-
ticipant in, and years ago, at that. In college. If it wasn't on the road
traveling, then at school. So really, he has nothing to be worried
about. It was good of Tom to arrange it—a generous friend who
gives much of himself.

The only thing is that he's so skinny. At his strongest, though he
had been doping, he had weighed nearly two hundred pounds.
Now he is afraid to step on a scale. Plus, it has been a long time, a
year almost, since he's been with someone.

After a few minutes, a woman comes into the waiting room—
slim, pale skin, straight red hair pulled back into a ponytail. She is
wearing black pants and a black T-shirt. Her breasts are small. She
is thirty maybe. The body of a dancer. She says something to the
man in a foreign language, moves to look over the counter at the appointment book, and turns to Cody and says his name.

———

They walk down a short hallway. Paintings of flowers are hung on lime cinder block. The room she brings him to is dark and warm and there is one table covered in thin white sheets. One of the walls is a floor-to-ceiling mirror. She says that Cody can get undressed to his underwear, or get totally nude if he likes, whichever he is most comfortable with. Though nude is better, easier. He can put his clothes on the floor, near a tan wood bureau, upon which sits a CD player, towels, several jars of what Cody assumes are oils or moisturizers.

"I'll leave you," she says.

Alone in the room, he doesn't know, at first, whether he ought to get totally nude, but decides finally that he should. It's right, he thinks. Appropriate.

He folds his coat and jeans and shirt and boxer shorts and places them upon his shoes. And he looks at himself in the mirror for a moment, though he is afraid that the girl will come in and see him doing this. Looks at himself and thinks, *Jesus Christ*. He looks like he did when he was fourteen. He has what they called "addict hips." His cock looks gray. Even in the low light, he can see every ridge in his sternum, as if, like dough, someone had pressed their thumbs into the breastbone. He turns his torso a bit and there is the scar on his elbow—a short, fat scar.

He pulls back the sheets, exposing the tan upholstery of the table. He realizes this is wrong, that he ought not lie upon this, and so turns one sheet back down. He slides in and places the other sheet high up on his chest, and then turns over onto his front.

He is concerned—the white sheet is so thin—she'll see everything. He presses the side of his face into the cushioned headrest, which itself is covered with a thin white cloth. The room seems to be roasting, and he worries that sweat will begin to accumulate on his back.

She knocks on the door and he starts to say "Come in" but just says "Co—" because his throat catches. She does come in. He can't see her at all. All he can see is the dark carpeting. He closes his eyes.

"Are you comfortable?" she asks.

"Yes," he says.

"I'm going to start," she says. "If it's too strong, or too soft, then let me know, okay?"

"Okay."

She turns on the CD player, and it's what? New Age? Nature? The sound of water washing up on a shoreline. She takes the sheet on his back and folds it down, much too far, he thinks, all the way past his hips, so that he is sure his ass is exposed, or at least mostly. Then there is the sound of her rubbing her hands together. Dry hands, it sounds like. Covering them with the oil. Then suddenly—it *seems* very sudden—they are on his back.

She presses hard. He can feel the texture of her fingertips. She kneads his shoulders and his back, spreading her hands out from his spine in the direction of his arms. God, his spine must look like a string of beads. It's like she's trying to peel the muscle off the bone. She may do it, he thinks. At one time, she would never have been able. He used to have such a back. Looked like a swimmer, had an eight-inch drop.

"Is it okay?" she asks. The cushion around his face—he can't speak. She must be able to feel him tensing, for she lightens up.

"I'll go softer," she says, and he says thank you.

Her hands are always on him—she never ceases to maintain contact. She works her way down his back, down his spine, both pushing and carving away at the muscle, then all the way to his buttocks. Near the small of his back, she presses down and molds her hands around until she is practically clutching his hip bone. He is sweating—he knows this now, for sure.

Will she say something? he wonders. Or will she just go for it? He supposes that either would be fine, though better if he didn't have to say anything.

She flattens and massages the area around his lower back for five minutes, maybe ten. She slides her hands up his back crosswise, her palms flat and slow, seeming to try to turn him over, though he understands that he is not to move. He feels, however, as if he is spinning. His face is damp.

He can hear her breathing. It's deliberate. She inhales as she presses down, exhales as she releases. It's practiced, learned.

She grabs his arms and, as if they are very heavy, lowers them from his side, where they rest on the table, so that they hang perpendicular to the floor. She stands very close to him—he can feel the warmth off her, though it is already so hot.

Her standing there so close to him, he wants to raise his arms and bring her into him. It would be very natural. Press his face into her. Though he doesn't.

It smells like what? Almond. Almond and citrus. A fragrance made from a poultice, liquefied, touched on her neck and wrists. It's not overwhelming. Is it coming from her? Perhaps. He breathes in deeply. The music is disorienting—he feels as if he is no longer in the city. Things are beginning to give themselves up, slough off.

She slides her hands from his armpit down to his wrists. He is afraid she will ask him about the scar on his elbow. It seems that a masseuse might know better, but it's just so obvious. What's this? How did this happen? He would have to tell her.

He was a baseball player. A pitcher. A long time ago, in college. Anyhow, the injury ruined his career.

From his wrists, she grabs his hands—the ball of his palm, the pad of his thumb—then pushes the blood down to his fingertips, which feel as if they're going to burst. She grabs each finger and tugs. Then she does something very strange, which is that she takes her own hand, her own fingers, and twines them between his. She goes back and forth.

This, he realizes, is something different. It's not part of what he might have expected. This means something. It's not nothing. She moves over to his left arm and repeats it, ending by lacing her fingers around and through his. He can't imagine her doing the same thing to Tom. No. This is about him. She saw his body and maybe she liked it, or perhaps she could *picture* what it once might have looked like and maybe could again. Or his face. Something. It's a way of saying what she can't say aloud. Really, this is the only way she would do it, he thinks now. Of course. A gesture.

He can receive this gesture, return it. As if to say, Yes, I understand. Tell me everything, and I'll tell you. She'd explain, of course, how she came to this country. Her parents still abroad. Her here, working as a masseuse, and maybe going to school in the evenings. Then she would ask him. He followed his buddy Tom out here when he moved back for a job. Yeah, you know him. He's a good guy and a good friend. Loyal. I don't need to tell you that.

She would want to know where he came from and he would say. His folks had passed before he came. Passed? Well—died. Yes. His father shortly after his mother. They were older. His mom was thirty-nine when she had him, his dad well into his fifties. His dad had once himself been a baseball player, a long time ago. His parents had owned a nursery, which, when they had grown ill, Cody had taken over.

Cody doesn't take her hand. He waits. She rests a hot towel on his back and wipes off the oil that she has rubbed on him.

"You can turn over," she says.

She touches his shoulders as if she is inserting an acupuncture needle—very carefully, only with her fingers. Now, she means. He knows that when he does this, she will be able to see right through the sheet. Well, what of it? Perhaps—could it be—it has been more than a year. God, he thinks, it might be two. It was as if after he arrived he simply turned over life to his work. The city was wide and gray. Winter was endless. So what if she sees him this way?

His legs are together. His arms at his sides. She centers him, as if she is preparing him for some remarkable event. And she begins to rub his chest. Too much bone, he thinks. She pushes harder. It feels as if she is going to rip open his breastbone, the way she tugs at the muscle. She seems to be pushing the blood down to his arms. He's turned on. How could one not be? She rubs in small circles below his rib cage, as if she is washing out his stomach. Then lower, near his belly button. It doesn't tickle, but he does tense a bit. She is very close. He knows what he must look like: the pale skin, thin waist, hip bones out like blades. So different from before. There was a time—it was only a few years ago—when he was so strong, so fit, that water would collect between the cubes of muscle in his abdomen.

He was nineteen, twenty. He was going to be drafted. He could feel himself near it—near the beginning of his life. To celebrate, he had taken a weekend trip with Tom, who was very good but never great, and never had any illusion that baseball would be his life.

On that trip he, along with about twenty other young men and women they had met up with, partied for two nights at Lake Havasu. Spring break. He must have fucked five girls that weekend. It was nothing new. Mostly, they drank. They lay out on a pontoon Tom had arranged for them. The sun on his body, searing him. It felt wonderful. At times they drifted under the orange rock and other times it seemed they were in the middle of a great body of water, an ocean, even. His skin swelled.

What went on, all those college kids—well, it was obscene, but he recalls thinking that he was young and that this was something to be enjoyed as best he could, that it might not last forever. There was the possibility that such a life might continue if he stayed healthy, but that was never assured.

In the afternoon of the second day, when the lake was most crowded with partygoers, and the state troopers trolled about in small boats, loudspeakers in their hands like guns, they neared a Sea Ray (whose name was *My Darling Clementine*), where other boats had gathered. Cody was sleeping on the deck, with Tom beside him. They were very close—their shoulders touched and also their wrists. A guy they knew from school came up to Tom.

"Well, well," he said. "Here lies the king of the Jews. Listen, you guys need to check this out."

Cody didn't want to. Tom turned over.

"I think you're going to want to see this."

They got up. Cody stood beside Tom near the railing of the pontoon.

And they all of them watched while a girl, completely nude, with a tattoo of a small black scorpion on her left hip, masturbated with an empty Miller Lite bottle. The kids cheered. When she was finished, she stood up and very gently, as if she were handing over a garland, tossed the bottle to Cody. He caught it. Held it up like a torch. Their friend said, *Hang on, hang on!* and snapped a Polaroid.

Cody saved it, wrote on the bottom *Lake Havasu, Spring Break*, kept it on the refrigerator in his apartment until he graduated, not having been drafted, but instead injured permanently; then at home for the brief time after college, keeping his parents' nursery; and now on his desk, displayed for people to see, the way one would keep and display a photograph of having caught a marlin.

"It doesn't hurt?" she asks, and he says no. "It feels good," he adds.

"Good," she says.

She continues to press upon his belly but does not pull the sheet off. She is going to wait. It makes the act more real. Then she folds the sheet over, exposing his left leg. She presses into his thigh and then his knee and then his calf. His calf the most. First around it, and then long, slow motions lengthwise. Then the top of his foot. Then between his toes. The smell of her—he wants to ask.

The same for his other leg. Again, she only nearly exposes him. After, she steps away, and when she comes back, she places another hot towel on his legs, cleaning them of the residue her hands left.

Finally, she stands to the right of him and tugs on his arm, the once-famous arm, almost as if she's trying to pull it out of the socket, then curls her hands around his shoulder and then his bicep and then his forearm. Certainly she can see the scar. Like it's glowing.

At last, again, she works her fingers through his. What a dear gesture. It says that she would take him even like this. Even at your leanest. It doesn't matter about before. Certain failures and—why

not just say it?—unluckiness. How he came here. There was nothing left in Arizona for him.

Well, it was just that his dad was senile. And his mom had had
cancer. He and his dad couldn't take care of her, so she had been staying in a facility. Cody was running the nursery for them. Sure it was
hard. It was a time when life was just a long episode, unending. Until
the instant he decided to leave. Yes, there really was a moment.

It was a Sunday. They had called about his mother. They had told
Cody to bring his dad to see her. It was the end and they needed to be
with her. He went home to get his dad, and he said to him, "Dad, we
gotta go see Mom. We gotta go say good-bye." And his father looked
at him. He knew who he was. It wasn't that he didn't know.

His father said that Karen was in New York now with her new
husband.

"No, Dad," he said. "Your *other* wife. Your second wife. My mom.
Emily. We have to go see her now."

His father said no. He wasn't going to do that. Instead, he would
write her a letter. It scared Cody, because he didn't know if his dad
knew how to write any longer. He might just scribble. That's what
happens, he would explain.

They argued for a little but it was no use—his father wasn't going
to go. So Cody got him a pen and a piece of paper from inside the
desk and his father wrote, and when he was finished, he folded the
letter three ways and gave it to Cody and said that he could go now,
and then asked him what time they were leaving to go to his game.

"I'm going to see Mom, Dad. Baseball is over."

"What was your ERA? What was it at the end, there?"

Cody told him. His father smiled.

"Good boy."

"Yes," he said, and he left to drive to see his mom. Only, along
the way he stopped. Pulled off the highway. The mountains blue in
the late afternoon. He got out of the car and opened the letter and
read it.

The letter said how his dad was very sorry that she was sick, and that he wasn't able to go see her at the hospital. He apologized for having banged up the car—though Cody didn't know what he was referring to. He explained that it was going to be okay, and *more* than okay, it was an exciting time, because when she got home from the hospital with Cody, they were going to start a new part of their lives. He wrote that he looked forward to spending the next thirty or forty or, God willing, fifty years, raising Cody and running a good business. He said that he loved her very much and that he would see her soon.

She circles her thumb around his palm and then simply grazes her palm against his. Then she brings her fingers into his, the same as before. He's glad that he's waited. He clasps his fingers around hers and sits up. He brings his left hand over his right, which is still holding hers, and covers her hands, as if they are making an oath. He looks at her.

"Oh," she says.

She is not surprised, but it's clear that there has been some mistake. Her face is calm. In the dim light, she looks older than he first thought. Perhaps even forty. He can make out the upper line of the cup of her bra.

"I thought—" he says.

"Oh. No. That's just one of the—" she begins, though it's clear she doesn't want to embarrass him. "Lie back. We're almost done," she says. "Do you want me to continue?"

"Yeah," he says. "I'm sorry."

"Lie back," she says, and he does, though now it's as if she's nearing the end of a haircut, evening things out. She does his left arm very quickly. She brings another towel over to him and cleans off his chest and arms.

"That's it. It's warm in here," she says casually.

"Yes," he says.

"You can get dressed now," she says. "Thank you."

She is already gathering her things, leaving the room.

He sits up. His clothes in the corner of the room, piled there, like something a tramp might leave after squatting in an alley. He dresses, though even this seems to take a kind of strength he doesn't possess.

He walks down the small hallway. He feels as if he might faint. In the waiting room, the man at the counter is on the phone. He's afraid that the man will say something to him. Correct him. *This is not that kind of place,* he would say. *Maybe you do that at some other kind of place, but not here.*

But the man doesn't say that. He gets off the phone and with what seems like warmth, kindness, even, he says that everything is already paid for.

"Happy birthday. From"—he is looking closely at the register—"Tom. Happy birthday from Tom. How old are you?" he asks.

In a way, Cody feels good. In spite of all. His body, at least, and that is something. Clean. Wrought. Purified.

"How old would you say I was?" he asks the man. Gray-blue light sinks from the stairwell, like snow piled up after a storm. He has very little right now, but that simply means he has much to gain.

"I don't know." The man smiles and hesitates. "I guess it would be hard to say."

There is another young man sitting in the same chair in which Cody sat while waiting for Helen. He is a lawyer probably, several years older than Cody but comfortable with his life, his place in the world. This is just part of his weekly routine. He knows Helen well. They talk about what they are doing for the weekend, which bars they've gone to, where they've eaten. Perhaps they have even seen each other out before.

Cody begins to walk out, and behind him, in the doorway, Helen appears. She's not ashamed. She says to the young man in the chair, "Come in."

CODE PINK

WHEN HE GETS a text message from his son that reads *I love you, Dad*, he's alarmed. He calls the son in California.

"Hey, Tom. I just got your note. I'm here at the office—well, I'm in and out all day. Okay. I'll talk to you soon. I hope you're well."

But the son doesn't call back. Not during a meeting that runs through the afternoon, not when the father has a drink with a lawyer with whom he is working on a very large transaction. Not on the long drive back to the suburbs from downtown.

He looks down at the phone resting in the burled wood tray (he drives a BMW 7 Series, massive) near the gearshift. Man-made lakes pass by him to the west. To the east, there are the Botanical Gardens.

At home, watching television, he asks his wife if she's spoken to Tom.

"No," she says.

"I think I'm going to call him," the father says, not adding that he's already done so.

"Okay, Stuart," the wife says. "Tell him hi for me."

They sit under vaulted ceilings so great that when they built the home, they tore down three giant oak trees in order to see the sky unobstructed. Some of the older neighbors complained.

He calls again and there is no answer. He doesn't leave a message. Before going to bed, he calls from the long bathroom heavy with marble, but again it goes to voice mail. It's an automated message, a woman telling him to press one or wait for the tone.

This is so like Tom—not to have even recorded a message.

"Hey, Tommy. Tomorrow, I think I'll be in and out again, but you can try me on the cell. We have that big meeting on Friday, so we're getting ready for that. Actually, better yet, you can leave a message with Felicia. She'll be around all day and she'll know where to get ahold of me. Well, either way. Good night."

Three in the morning, he reaches for the phone, lifts it, and puts it to his mouth.

"Tom?" he says. "Tom?"

His wife says quietly, "Stuart, what are you doing?"

"Tom?" he says again. "Tom." He opens his eyes. "I thought Tom was on the phone."

"No," she says. Her voice is light, a little irritated. She touches him on the shoulder. "Go back to sleep, Stuart."

He wakes at 5:30 A.M. He drives a few miles to their country club. It's summer. A man in a green shirt is bent over a sprinkler head in the great circular lawn before the entrance to the clubhouse. The grass is silver. The sun has not fully risen. Behind the club is the golf course—blue with the light just coming up.

The man stands, puts his hand to the small of his back, then waves. Stuart waves back. He has done this many times.

Inside, he walks by a composite of the club's board, of which he is a member. He was thirty pounds heavier in that picture.

They say Tom looks like him. Perhaps it is true, though he doesn't quite see it. Tom seems smaller, in a way, though they are both tall.

In the gym, he runs for an hour, up from twenty minutes when he first started working out, when Tom left. After, he goes outside to swim. The morning is cool, but the pool is heated. One woman is in the pool, tiny, she does the breaststroke. Her shadow looks like a jellyfish. Light is making the water glow. He watches her.

Tom spent two summers here lifeguarding. He saved two lives in that time—children who'd gone under, whom he resuscitated. There were rumors he slept with the assistant GM, a woman twenty-one years older than he, but he had never said anything to Stuart about that.

After he swims, he returns to his locker, checks his phone, again opens the text message. *I love you, Dad.* If Tom had called, just now or an hour ago, he would see it as a missed call, though in any event, it's only 4:00 A.M. in California now.

Tom will wake early, but only to surf. He's just picked it up, but he is quite good. He won a tournament, even. He sent pictures of himself wrapped in an unspeakably blue wave, hunched over a pink board. The sides of his torso, tensed, were like a horse's. Another picture of him with a girl so pretty, the men featured in the background were staring at her. Well, nothing was new about that. She was another in a long line.

Instead of returning home after college, Tom had remained out west for a few years. When he finally did come back (Stuart had wanted Tom to join him in his company, though Tom had said no, and so instead, Stuart got him a job at a friend's firm), he said he wasn't quite ready to think about graduate school, which both Stuart and his wife encouraged. Not yet, Tom would say. Maybe soon. He'd indicated that he was playing with the idea of business school: *It's definitely a possibility.* Stuart insisted he contact some people he knew, but Tom told him that it was okay. It seemed his official education was over. He had already learned much.

"Well, that's okay," Stuart said to him. He really didn't have to worry about it. Stuart and his wife celebrated him whenever they could.

During that period, Stuart would invite Tom to have cocktails with him after work downtown, before Tom went out with friends. He even invited him to his monthly card game with a few fellows from the neighborhood (these were lawyers or dermatologists or traders he'd grown friendly with over the years), though after attending a few, Tom said he thought his dad might just want to hang out with his buddies alone. Stuart suggested a book club, though picked books that *he* liked (Patrick O'Brien). Tom said why read about all these places but not see them? They played golf, but Tom was appeasing him.

When Stuart bought that BMW a few years ago, he took Tom to the dealership with him, and when the dealer invited Stuart into his office for the final negotiation, Stuart asked if Tom could come.

For an hour and forty-five minutes, Stuart haggled with the dealer. He watched Tom watching them. When he asked how much he could get the whole thing for, with the high-security feature included (it added nearly another ton, was totally useless, would delay its shipment, and he only did it to impress Tom), Tom got up to leave the office, saying he was going to get a pop.

One day, Tom decided all on his own to take what savings he had and move to California.

He announced this at dinner. It was nearing winter. The skylights were covered with snow. It would be dark for months.

His wife smiled and wanted to know why.

"I need—" Tom said, looking down. "I just—I think it's a smart move."

Stuart said nothing. Later, he wrote Tom a check for thirteen thousand dollars, but Tom wouldn't take it. He would find work; he always did. It happened very suddenly. Within a few weeks, he packed up his old Nissan Z, and he left.

At nine, Stuart meets with the vice president of a Big Four accounting firm for breakfast at the Drake. He has his phone in his pocket, and he reaches for it throughout their conversation to feel if it is vibrating.

The man has been trying to get a meeting with Stuart for months. He is trying to steal Stuart away from his current firm, for the man is aware of the pending transaction with which Stuart is involved. And he knows there is a son. In an effort to connect with Stuart, he discusses family.

The man has a daughter at Notre Dame, jokes about how she is a theater major, probably going for her Ph.D., surely bankrupting him. He laughs. It's funny. Money is not the issue. That is what one would think of the two men.

"You have a son, right?" he asks.

"Yes," Stuart says.

"Is he anything like mine?" the man asks. He is stirring cream into his coffee. The act seems violent, the clanking against the china as he places the teaspoon down, terribly loud in the quiet lobby. Stuart opens his phone, which is blank, and turns the volume up to its highest.

"Oh, I suppose not. I mean, when he was in high school and college, he was pretty focused on sports, but now," Stuart says, running his hand over his tie, like he's straightening it, "well—he's in California."

"Oh," the man says.

"He's taking classes there."

"That's nice," the man says.

"Yeah," Stuart adds, though that is all he will say.

The man sits up straight, looking at Stuart, holding the coffee cup in one hand, the saucer in the other. He has no reason not to believe him. He can even imagine Tom—big like Stuart, and quiet like him, too.

Which isn't typical. Stuart is not the arrogant CEO, unlike the type he has met many times. Stuart is tactile, sensitive—the humility of a man for whom success is not a foregone conclusion.

But Stuart seems distracted. Traffic is quieting on Lake Shore Drive, settling into the day. The man indicates that his firm may be better suited to handle Stuart's books. Stuart says perhaps. He is not unwilling to listen. They agree to be in touch.

In his office, he asks Felicia, a woman who has worked for him for twenty years, if Tom called.

"No," she says.

"Are you sure?" he asks.

"Yes," she says. Although she has heard nothing from Tom, she goes through the gesture of checking her e-mail so that Stuart can see. "Nothing. How is Tommy?"

"He's good. He had a question and I told him to call me at the office."

She has watched Tom grow up and she admires him. She knows, however, that he will never be the boy his father wants him to be, though Stuart is a fine man. When Tom was a little boy, Stuart would show him shop drawings of plots of land, designs for buildings under construction, but all Tom ever wanted to do was talk to Felicia, upon whose desk sat a number of snow globes. She had told him many times where each was from, but he always asked again when he would see her.

The transaction that is to be completed the following day is a land deal whereby Stuart will sell a massive parcel in Louisiana to an energy company that believes under it there is a sea of natural gas. Though he is already wealthy, wealthier than he had ever hoped, this deal will be what allows him to retire. They have decided.

It will set up him and his wife, and also Tom, for life. And the generation to follow. He will keep his business, but only so that Tom can begin a new iteration sometime in the future.

It has become, since the energy company first approached him two years ago, part of a design that seems both necessary and inevitable. Stuart sees himself and his wife gardening, he sees them at their country club, he sees himself lecturing to business school students, but above all he sees him and Tom.

Marlin fishing in the Caribbean. Golf at Augusta. The Bellagio. Tom will seek his counsel. Stuart will listen. He will not be prescriptive.

At his desk, he looks at his phone. The desk is thirty years old, bought when Stuart was thirty years old himself, a young husband with a child.

He took over a development company whose owner he had

worked for as a laborer on a job site, then as a field superintendent. The man was seventy-two and didn't have children. His wife had died. Stuart became his friend. He was deferential. He listened; the man had much to say. Naturally.

Within six months, Stuart was working in the office, distributing shop drawings, paying visits to job sites.

"You understand what it means to work. *Really* work," the man told Stuart. "Nobody understands that anymore."

The man wasn't senile, but close. He would say it a dozen times a day.

Within a year, he died, his business turned over to Stuart.

Stuart himself never graduated from college. He was from Jacksonville, Florida. He had dropped out of a junior college, served two years in the army as a supply clerk, then returned home, where he was a bouncer for a time. His own parents died, and he met the woman who would become his wife. Worked as a gardener, worked as a handyman. At night, they got drunk in the heat, were among friends but going nowhere—they were twenty-five, then thirty. The aimlessness he felt was like a sickness.

He took a job at a moving company, made delivery of another young couple's furniture in Chicago. He didn't return home. He told his wife to come meet him there.

He calls Tom again.

"Hey, Tom. It's Dad. Listen, I tried calling you earlier. I'm in the office today. So you can try me here. Or on the cell. I'll be home tonight. I know Mom would like to hear from you. Maybe—I was thinking—I could make a visit after this Louisiana thing goes through. I don't know. I'm just thinking out loud. Okay, Tom. I wanted to let you know."

Felicia comes in and reminds him that she needs signatures, and that his lawyer will meet him at the hotel tomorrow at 11:00 A.M.

"We have that party at Gibson's after, okay?" she says. "Diane said she was going to drive in for it."

"Okay."

"Are you all right, Stuart?"

"Yeah," he says. "Do you think—" he begins, but then stops.

"What?"

"Nothing."

"What?"

"I was just wondering. Do you know if this fella Phil has any kids?"

"Phil from the gas guys? I have no idea."

"I think he does. I think he's got a son at Michigan. He told me that. What about that other guy? Brian. From their Luxemberg office. What about him?"

"Oh, I don't know, Stuart," Felicia says. "Why do you ask?"

"I was just wondering. I just didn't want to bring it up if they didn't. Have kids. You don't know with this stuff. A month ago, I was at the grocery store. And there was this cashier. This black guy. And he asked the guy checking out in front of me how this guy's wife was. I guess he saw her often. The cashier mentioned something about when she was due. I guess she was pregnant. But the guy said that she'd miscarried. And he asked the cashier not to say anything about it when he saw the wife again."

"Oh," Felicia says.

"Anyhow," Stuart says, "I think I'll take this stuff home with me. I'll sign it all at home."

"You're taking off? You don't want to do that here? That way, I'll have it," she says.

"No. I'll bring it tomorrow."

"You know what," she says, "it'll take us no time to go through this, Stuart. Why don't we just knock it out, and then you don't have to worry about it."

Which means she won't have to worry about it. On the venture, she stands to make a great deal, as well.

"Tom didn't call?" he asks.

"No, Stuart," she says.

"Well, look, I'm going to head home. We're having an early dinner. I'll just go over these one final time and have it all ready for tomorrow."

"Okay," Felicia says. "Call me if you have any problems."

On the way home, he stops off at the Botanical Gardens. They've been members since Tom was born. At the entrance, he brings his window down.

"It's twenty dollars per car," the woman inside the gate says. She is his age. Pretty.

"We're actually members," Stuart says, but then realizes that his wife has the card, and the membership sticker is on her car. "My wife has it," he says, laughing a bit. "Maybe you can look us up?"

The woman frowns.

"You know what," she says, "our computers are down. Let me— you know what I'll do here," she says, and reaches for a walkie-talkie on the small desk. The heat rising from between the car and her small kiosk is tremendous. Stuart is sweating.

"That's okay," he says, and he takes out his wallet and gives her a twenty-dollar bill. She smiles. "I'm sorry," she says, and hands him a ticket to place on his dashboard.

When Tom was a little boy, they threw a birthday party for him here. Tom was ten. The children were in shorts and collared shirts. They adored Tom. He was in possession of distance, which is a form of power. He was like a celebrity who only sometimes made appearances. When they brought in his birthday cake, with frosting of baseballs and baseball gloves and tennis rackets and balls, the candles burning, Tom wasn't there.

Stuart found him outside, overlooking the koi pond. Tom was barely tall enough to see over the railing, but he stood on his tiptoes, arms out along the metal strip, as if he were thinking something very important, taking in the sun.

"Hey, pal. We're doing your birthday cake."

Tom didn't say anything.

"You gotta come in, buddy. Everyone is waiting."

"Dad?"

"Yeah." His wife was signaling wildly for him to get in. They were wasting time. There had been conversations about indulging Tom.

"How long do you think someone could breathe under there?"

He gets out of his car and walks to the entrance. It's quiet. The air is clear, however, and dry. Elderly women sit at the information desk, eager to give him a map. He smiles at them. He passes through the visitor center to the bridge that connects it to the rest of the garden. The water below is still, the arbor above covered with ivy. Though it is summer, it seems quiet.

In the rose garden, there is a middle-aged couple, a man wheeling his wife in a wheelchair. Fat bees hang in the air. Across the country, Stuart thinks, Tom might be in peril. Someone might have taken advantage of him, of his goodness.

In a tucked-away corner of the sensory garden, near a small hanging apiary, he sees a young man behind an ice-cream cart. The boy is older than Tom by a few years, a bit heavy, a thick red beard. His hair is curling out from under his green hat. There is a name tag that reads *Padraig*.

"Hi," he says to Stuart.

"Hi," Stuart says.

"Can I get you anything?"

"Um. No, that's okay."

"Okay," the boy says.

"Well, okay," Stuart says. "How about a Diet Coke?"

"You bet," the boy says.

He digs into the cooler. His arm is thick and covered with freckles. It's strange that they would set up a cart so near an apiary. Bees crawl in and out of small dark circles.

"You ever get stung?" Stuart asks the boy. He gives him two dollars. "Keep the change," he says.

"Thanks," the boy says. "You know, that was the first thing I asked when I found out I was going to be working next to this thing. But I haven't. Not once."

They are maybe ten feet from it. The afternoon sun is setting, shining on the boy's neck.

"You should collect hazard pay," Stuart says.

The boy leans over, setting his elbows on the sliding metal top.

"No joke," the boy says. "I hate bees. Seriously."

"Are you guys busy here?"

"Less so during the day," the boy says. "Mostly, it's senior citizens and retirees. The weekends are a shit show, though. Obviously."

Stuart feels old, paternal. He wants to find out why a boy would be working at a cart, selling soda and ice cream. This is a boy Tom would hang out with, a boy who plays the bass guitar.

"Is it fun?"

"It's okay. They have cooking demos during the day in the pavilion, and that's a blast."

"Huh, I didn't know that."

"Yeah. I'm a chef," the boy says.

"Really?"

"Yep. I go to culinary school downtown. And I work as a sous-chef too."

"Great," Stuart says. "You like working here?"

"Well enough. You know, it's just something. I mean, what the hell else would I be doing, right? And, I mean, I'm able to help with the demos sometimes, so that's good. You know, connections."

"I do," Stuart says.

"Overall, it's good," the boy says.

The boy then stands up and raises his arms into the air, stretching. As he does this, his shirt lifts, revealing a thick paunch, red hair spread over it. He yawns and releases his arms, bringing them down, and smacks a bee with his knuckles. The boy jumps a bit when he sees it, grabbing his hand as if he's been stung. The bee bounces off his hand, buzzes around Stuart and the boy, crawling back into the apiary.

"Jesus!" the boy says. "God! I hate bees. Man! It's just a matter of time. I gotta get them to move this thing. I'm probably allergic. I'm sure I am."

The boy hops from one foot to another, bending his knees. He looks at the apiary as if he's trying to figure out how to take it down.

"Well, I suppose when you move on to something a bit more regular, you won't have to worry about it."

The boy perks up at this, focusing on Stuart.

"What do you mean 'regular'?"

"Well, I mean—you know, like a regular job."

"What's *that* look like?" the boy asks.

"You know. An office. A desk. Computer. Regular."

"Why the hell would I want that?" the boy says. "I told you, I'm a chef."

"Oh," Stuart says. "Okay. I'm—that's okay."

He begins to back away. The boy stands there, straightening, obstinate, setting his baseball cap firmly on his head. Another bee flies out from the apiary, passing under the brim of the cap. The boy backs away, waving his hand fiercely.

"*Fuck!*" he says. "Goddamn bees."

Stuart turns, passing by a tangle of willow leaves, walking away from the boy, past the apiary, checking the small metal plate fixed on its side, which reads: *To Tom, Upon Your Graduation. Love, Mom and Dad.*

For dinner they meet with another couple. He is a doctor—an allergist. She teaches third grade. They eat at a steak house in the suburbs near them. They have known the couple fifteen years. Stuart likes the man, though they would never, on their own, make a plan to get together.

For a time, they talk about tomorrow's meeting. It's no secret, and Stuart's wife has told friends excitedly. The doctor says that it will be nice to have time, of course, but even more important, the ease, the soft coming down of a long, hard-earned career.

Yes, Stuart agrees. His wife smiles, puts her head down a bit.

Stuart asks after the couple's kids. One working for the CDC in Atlanta, one doing Doctors Without Borders in Uganda.

The man is huge, nearly 250 pounds. Strange, Stuart always thought, that a doctor would be so heavy. He smokes, too. The doctor explains, as he orders salmon, that he is on a new diet. One pound at a time, he says.

"How did you do it?" he asks Stuart. "You must have lost twenty pounds," he says. "You look like a forward. Isn't it true?" the doctor says to his wife.

"Yes," she says. "Really something."

Stuart explains his exercise routine, the running followed by the swimming, but doesn't say that it wasn't until Tom left that he'd started. Standing on the scale at the club—it was a kind of degradation. A thinning. He was no longer hungry.

Tom and he would speak once a week at first, then every other week, then once a month. It had started to become too much for Stuart. Tom's voice was growing quieter. Stuart sent him a new phone. Their conversations became more and more brief, Tom's sentences more truncated. *That's great, Dad. You bet. No problem.* What did they have out there? Nothing. Nothing that he couldn't enjoy here. Stuart would have ensured it if it meant he would have stayed.

The entrées are served. The doctor tells a story. He was at the hospital today. He is eating while talking. Stuart can see in his mouth.

"We had a code pink," the doctor says. "The first I've seen since— Jesus—" he says, "since my residency at Rush. Twenty-five years ago."

"A what?" Stuart asks.

"A code pink. It's when a baby goes missing from the nursery."

"What do you mean?" Stuart asks.

"Someone stole a baby," he says, the back of his tongue smeared with salmon, like a paste. Stuart can smell it.

"What do you mean?" Stuart asks. His wife looks up, her face solemn.

"Yeah. Someone came in and stole the baby out of the nursery."

"Aren't there people watching?"

Stuart's wife puts her hand on his wrist, which is holding a steak knife as wide as a trowel.

"Yeah. But it happens. Not often, of course."

"Who was it?"

"Um. I think it turned out to be the sister-in-law."

"She—she just went in and took it?"

"Yeah. It was a hell of a scene. The police came."

"Jesus," Stuart says. "Jesus."

"It was close, too," the doctor explains. "The woman was in the parking lot. It was just a matter of minutes. She almost got away."

Stuart puts his fork and knife down. He looks at the ceiling. Tom. Tommy. The vision of him in light blue surfer shorts. His body, he was getting bigger—the torso of a running back he never bothered to achieve.

"Almost," the doctor says. "A day old."

Stuart excuses himself. Near the men's room, he looks at his phone. It's dark. He calls Tom, but there is still no answer. He calls again.

"Tom," he says—his voice is thin. "It's Dad. Please—" he starts. He hangs up.

Pulling into their driveway, Stuart opens the garage door.

"I'm going to leave the car outside," he says.

"Why?" his wife asks.

"I don't know. I may move some stuff around in the garage. Go ahead. I'll be in in a few minutes."

"Okay," she says. "I spoke with Felicia, by the way. She wanted to know that you're all set for tomorrow."

"You bet," he says.

He waits for her to close the door to the interior of the home. It rides back for half an acre—a home that seems to have annexed wing after wing. Tom's room is in the back, against thick shrubs.

The car is cool, the engine still on, running low. Stuart puts his fingers on the steering wheel. The phone in his pocket, he waits for it to ring, as if he can will it.

All of Tom's things sit in the back of the garage. A massive tennis bag, a Louisville Slugger bag full of baseball bats, a container with three basketballs, dozens of two- and three-tiered trophies that Tom himself removed from his room, replaced with books with titles like the *The Chomsky-Foucault Debate* and *A Theory of Justice,* as if he were ridding himself of all that he'd accomplished. Which was foolish. Foolish and, moreover, selfish. Few had the opportunities that Tom had.

His heartbeat has slowed these months since Tom left. It is a metamorphosis into something cold-blooded, something geological, without heart but still functioning; the attending features of a man— one says, *Look at his home. Look at his wife. Look at the car. His son? . . . Oh. You didn't know?*

He takes the phone out. He just looks at it. Small, black—he would crush it if not for the message it contains, which he must keep, consider, marvel at—damning.

"Tom. It's Dad," he says firmly. "Listen, Tom, you can't just—you can't leave a message like this and not pick up the phone. We're out of our minds here. Your mother. This message you wrote me. I mean— Jesus. I don't know what you're doing. I just don't. You have to come back here, Tom. You just do. You have to come back. You have to come home. There's nothing out there. It's fucking ridiculous, Tom. This time, it is. You mustn't do this to us. Why aren't you answering? Will you pick up the goddamn phone, Tom? Please. I'm not yelling, but please. I'm coming out there, Tom. I'm going to come to you. You don't have to— I'm going to be there soon, okay? Please pick up the phone. Answer it. Answer it. I'm coming to get you. It's going to be okay. Dad is coming. Your father is coming. Just stay put. Please. Please, don't go anywhere, Tom. Stay where you are and I'll be there as soon as I can. I love you, okay? I just—I do. I love you. I'll see you in a few hours."

————

He waits until his wife goes to sleep. Near midnight, from the library, he calls up one airline and asks for the next flight out to Los Angeles. There is none, the woman tells him. Not until tomorrow.

"I can be there in an hour," he says.

"I'm sorry," she says.

"It's an emergency," he says.

"I'm sorry, sir," she says again.

He calls another. He has to work through several automated menus. He feels sick. He feels as if he is already moving out of his body. He is thin. He thinks of Tom. Stuart is divining him from across the country, imagining him. Tom is so strong, but his circumstances are perilous, too great even for him.

This other woman says the same thing—no flight until tomorrow. Well, he'll pay anything. It doesn't matter. A third airline—there *is* a flight, connecting from the East Coast and arriving around three in the morning, but it will cost him three thousand dollars. Fine, he says, and she asks for his credit card number and he gives it to her and she asks where he wants to sit and he says anywhere.

He doesn't pack. He gathers his keys and his wallet.

He walks toward the door. From the dining room, which looks out onto the yard, is the long driveway; in the middle, the car.

Nearly nine thousand pounds, can run on flat tires, can eject oil slicks, windows that an AK-47 couldn't penetrate. He was told it would withstand a hand grenade. It takes up most of the driveway, wide and low. On either side are long rows of pansies, which Stuart himself planted, violet and white in the daytime, black as shells at night.

OUR HERO DAVID KATZ

CHRISTMASTIME. The streets are quiet, the lake black. Tom has returned home for a visit. It is his gift to me.

"You see that bellhop near the door?" Tom asks.

"Sure," I say.

"He's the one who tells the escorts who their client will be for the night."

"Bullshit."

"No kidding, Robbie. You know that G-20 thing they had a few years ago? There were *ten* bellhops where he's standing. Two just for the Turks. Those guys. Jesus. They go up there, tell them a phony name, Kemal Ataturk or whatever, and *boom,*" he says, shaking his head, turning back to his drink.

"Maybe," I say.

"Look," he says. "Wait an hour. In an hour or so, you're going to see a woman go up to him. She's not parking her car, and she's not checking into the hotel. You'll know who she is. Believe me. See for yourself. You've got the money."

I do believe him, and I do have the money. I look over to the bellhop. He's standing by the revolving door. He's wearing a red uniform, thick leather gloves, a gold nameplate. He's standing under a wreath as big as a rocket. His face is mild. He looks at us.

"Just what I need, Tom. Is it true about those Turkish guys?"

"Oh sure," he says. "Are you joking? Do you *know* what they're into over there?" He takes a sip of his beer. "I knew this guy—*well,*" he says, chuckling to himself, "*knew* is not really the right word. But this guy could tell you a thing or two about the Turkish. He was an interesting figure. I told you about this kid I went to grad school with—Sam? Him and his brother? Did I ever tell you this one?"

"Maybe," I say. "Yeah, I think—"

He raises his hand; he nearly chokes on his beer.

"No, no. You would have remembered this. I mean, this was something else."

Tom in business school at UCLA. It's three guys: Tom, this other guy, Blake, a former hotshot golfer from the University of Texas, and this guy Sam. Sam Katz. This little Jewish guy. Yale under- grad. Smart as hell—he was there on the school's dime.

They noticed him at the welcome reception. He stood in the cor- ner, drinking Coke the whole time, talked to no one, but in class, you could ask him anything, he'd give you chapter and verse. Tom and Blake figured they'd do well with a guy like that in their study group.

At first, Tom's a little nervous. The whole school enterprise feels like a commitment. But with some help from his dad, he managed to get in, and believed he wanted the money that would come after.

Pretty quickly, they all figure things out. The three of them get some good work done that first year. Soon enough, Tom and Blake realize that it's going to be okay. They're starting to relax a little more. They recognize that they're going to make it. At the very least, they're going to get by.

And most important, they have old Sam. Sam Katz. Their ace in the hole.

The thing with Sam, Tom explains, was that he was the nicest guy you'd ever want to meet. You wouldn't know it at first, because he was so quiet and a little strange—the type of guy who couldn't really look you in the eye. Something was a little off about him. But he was really smart. And nice. Short, losing his hair at twenty-six, dark around the eyes, glasses. Every so often, they'd invite him out. Sort of as a joke, but not entirely—a party was a party to these guys. They didn't care who went, or how they looked.

Once that first year, Sam went with them. It wasn't pretty, Tom says. He lasted about an hour. A girl came to talk to him—she was just asking for directions to a nearby restaurant—he nearly wet himself. Later, after Sam left, Tom slept with her. Anyhow, he was a good guy.

Come their second year, they have a good rhythm going. Sam prepares the cases that they go over during their study sessions. He's happy to do it for them. He makes copies and he'll even annotate the thing. It's almost the end of the first semester, nearing Christmas.

They're at a coffee shop, studying, and Blake is checking his e-mail, and he starts complaining about how his fiancée, this girl Laura, keeps sending him these offers for deals on vacations to Kenya. She won't stop with the e-mails.

Sam says, sort of out of nowhere, that when they're there, they should check out a restaurant called Carnivore. Blake asks how Sam knows the place. Sam says his brother. David.

"David's the one you should ask, if you want the inside scoop. They have a great music scene. And *great* food. I hear," he says, looking back down.

Here's the thing: As far as Tom and Blake knew, Sam Katz was an only child. They're surprised. I mean, they weren't best friends, but you would think you would know if a guy had a sibling. I mean, they knew where he was from—Chappaqua, New York. They knew where he had gone to high school—Horace Greeley. They even knew his favorite book—*The Magic Mountain*. They had seen pictures of his folks. They had studied at his place. He had even cooked for them once. Last year, around the same time, he'd made latkes for them. The kid even bought them Hanukkah gifts and gave them gelt.

This is what Tom means when he says "the nicest guy you'd ever want to meet."

But they couldn't remember his having mentioned a brother. It seemed strange. It was hard, in a way. It wasn't like when you were in college and you had all this time to get to know people. They had this little triumvirate, and they thought they knew one another, but it was clear they were only semifriends. Really, Tom explains, it was a lonely time. I'm surprised to hear him say this.

So, Tom says straight out, "I didn't know you had a brother, Sam."

"Sure," he says. "David. He's nine years older than me."

"Well," Blake says, giggling, not sure what to make of the whole thing, "how does *he* know this place?"

"He lived there for a couple years. He was a foreign service officer."

"What?" Tom asks.

"He worked for the State Department," Sam says, leaning back in his chair.

"Wait, so you have a brother, David? And he lives in Kenya?" Tom asks.

"Well, he *was* stationed there. Now he's in New York. He's out of federal service."

"What do you mean 'federal service'?" Tom asks.

"Oh—" Sam says, as if Tom has made some kind of faux pas. "He's in the private sector now. In New York. He's with a firm there."

Tom and Blake aren't sure what to make of this, but they sense that they are on to something important. They begin to ask questions of Sam.

The biography of David Katz was a little spotty in places, Tom says, but it was—well, it was something.

Apparently, while Sam went to regular public school, David, who was a magnificent fuckup (hard to imagine if he was related to Sam), went to military school. If he had some behavior problems going in (apparently, according to Sam, he was balling everything by the age of fourteen), he didn't when he was finished. He'd had a pretty hard time his freshman year, but he was flying straight when he was done.

Instead of going to Yale (Sam's dad was a legacy there), which he had the grades for, David went to West Point. He did a tour in Iraq, where he was a Delta operator, and then went to work for the State Department, where he was a foreign service officer.

That's where things start to get a little unclear for Blake and Tom, and this night, the night at the coffee shop, Sam's not saying any more. It's just something he's mentioned. He goes back to reviewing the cases. He lifts the mug to his lips slowly. He sips. He looks at Blake and Tom. They don't talk much more that night about David, at least not in front of Sam.

But on the drive back to where Tom and Blake live, they say how strange it is that they didn't know the guy had a brother. But maybe, they think, it's not so strange. Because, why *would* they know? There is no rule that says you have to know these things. They start to piece it together.

Tom acknowledges here that it was a little silly, but in a way— well. Perhaps I could understand? He felt that possibilities were narrowing, when his whole life is premised on possibility. They wanted to have a little fun.

They stop off at Blake's.

Laura, Blake's fiancée, wants Tom to go home; it's late. "Can you guys *please*—" she says, but they have some serious investigating to do. "This is important!" Blake says. They do some research. What is the State Department trying to do in Kenya? they wonder. What the heck would a guy like David Katz be doing there?

Blake gets them drinks. A professional recreator, Blake is. He brings out a hidden glass pipe, which Tom fills.

What they figure is that when Sam said that David was "a foreign service officer," what he *really* meant was that his brother was a spy. That's why he never said anything about him. And why Kenya? Well—and they look this up—Muslims. Extremists funneling into the country from the Horn of Africa, from Somalia into Kenya.

Which was terrific, Tom explains, because here's this guy, David Katz, this super-Jew, spying on the Muslims! They sit at Blake's apartment for the rest of the night, getting drunk, smoking weed that Blake's fiancée doesn't approve of and makes very clear to them she's not happy about. It's two in the morning, and she's opening windows loudly and slamming doors. She is gorgeous; she is ready to murder him. But they're filling in the gaps about David.

The semester comes to a close. Tom goes home to see his parents and to party with old friends. Blake and his fiancée attend a series of weddings. Sam stays at school, they think, but he mentions going home to New York, how he'll probably see David.

They think of him alone there. It must have been hard. Tom says he didn't like to think of it. Sam was the last guy who was going to get a piece in that city. Blake says how maybe it'd be nice if his brother came out to pay him a visit.

"Yeah," Sam says. "Maybe I'll mention it to him."

They come back the next term. They start up right away with their little group. This time, however, Sam suggests, and Blake and Tom quickly agree, to meet up at Sam's place. It's quieter. Blake has the fiancée and Tom lives with a bunch of other guys. In any event, over the winter, Blake and Tom have decided they need to dig further.

Sam's place is a characterless studio not far from the school. Inside, it's just this little futon with this lame plaid comforter. An old sofa. There is no television. An old CD player. There is a laptop that looks like it weighs thirty pounds. He's got one picture of his folks on the nightstand by the bed—they look like nice people. There is a painting, a Chuck Close knockoff, that you could tell Sam made in a high school or a college art class. There is a small bonsai tree on the Ikea table. Over his bed, and the thing Tom remembers most: the Eagles 1976 *Hotel California* poster.

Blake and Tom, who are kind of big guys, sit on this sofa, and Sam himself sits, back perfectly erect, in a folding chair across from them. Sam asks them if they are hungry. He has made food. He brings out from this galley kitchen some cookies. They eat. For a while, they study. Sam gives them all an agenda for the evening. He directs the session. He seems less deferential.

After about an hour, though, Tom and Blake can't really bear it, and Blake asks about David.

"So, did you see David when you were at home?" Blake asks, smiling, looking at Tom. "Did he finally come out to visit his little brother?"

"No," Sam says wearily. "No, he was traveling. He was in Europe."

"Work?" Blake asks.

"Yeah," Sam says. He goes to get them—and this is a first—some beer. He brings it in from the fridge. He also brings out a bunch of frosted mugs from the freezer. "He travels *all* the time. He was in Amsterdam when I was at home. We hardly ever see each other," though, he adds, they are very close.

"Amsterdam? What was he doing there?" Tom asks. They all eat cookies and drink beer. Old Sam has outdone himself.

"He was working on some kind of merger. There's a—well, I can't say a *ton* about it, but there's a biomed company in Seattle that's interested in acquiring a smaller firm there."

Tom and Blake are disappointed.

"But he sent me some pictures," Sam says.

"Can we see?" Tom asks.

Sam goes into his desk. There are some printouts of pictures and some regular photos. Some are street shots at night—the Golden Bend, the bridges and the canals lit up, pictures of a group of very good-looking men drinking at outside patios. Tom and Blake look closely.

"Which one is your brother, Sam?"

"The one on the end," he says, pointing with a pale, hairy-knuckled pinkie.

The picture is grainy. The man seated, in a fine blue suit, could very well be Sam's brother. You can't tell how tall he is. His hair is nearly shaven against his head. He is tan. His arms are around two women—they look local, European, but what does a girl from the Netherlands look like? Tom and Blake don't know. One is seated on his lap. David's tie is undone. The table is covered with empty beer glasses.

"It's funny, the way they do it over there," Sam says casually, taking the photos back, "is that they make you shower first. You believe that? You go to one of these places, and they have a shower. Right there in the room. Well, they have other customs in other places, of course, but David got a kick out of that. I—you guys would really like it there."

"Wait," Tom says, "how did he even get into this kind of work?"

"He went to business school after his government work," Sam says.

"Where?"

It was exactly where they'd expected, Tom explains.

That night, they break early. They need drinks. They need to digest.

They invite Sam out with them. He agrees. Before he leaves, he changes. It was funny, Tom explains. He put on this leather jacket. It wasn't Members Only, but close. He had on light blue jeans, tapered near the ankles. White socks. Well, what difference did it make to them? None.

"Just a decent guy," Tom says.

They drive to a bar. Sam in the backseat, smiling. Probably the most fun he's had in his life, though it's just a regular night for Blake and Tom. They want to hear more, and Sam feeds them little bits of information.

For example, Sam explains that because David travels so much, and the company he works for does so much business with the airline, he'll go to the airport and a concierge will approach him in the lounge, inviting him to board the plane early. It's like not even traveling, Sam explains.

David will lie back in his seat, hot towels bloating the skin on his hands. The empty plane, fueled, ready to launch across the Atlantic, winter coming down around the giant fuselage, the entire world seems cold, cold even that night in L.A.; and outside, at the gate, people are waiting for their rows to be called, checking their tickets, frustrated, harried. But not David Katz.

David, as Tom imagines it, is resting comfortably. He's young. He dozes; he dreams. His body is like a blade. He's earned this, Tom feels, and if *earned* is not the right word, then *deserves* is. With what he'd have done in the army, and all that he did later—it would really be impossible to say.

At the bar, they sit in a circle over a low table. Blake and Tom lean in. Sam gets a drink. He waits. He's had a few at this point. Maybe he's tired of talking about David. Well, it'd be understandable, and in any event, there's only so much he's at liberty to say.

"This is David's favorite," Sam says. He's drinking a Höegarden. "David says that they drank this by the bootful in the Green Zone." Sam puts his hands on his stomach, which is distended.

"That must have been hard for you," Blake says. His phone vibrates. It's his fiancée, but he ignores it. "For him to be there. You must have worried a lot." He's genuine.

"Yeah," Sam says.

"I mean, it sounds like it was pretty dangerous."

"Oh, it *was*. It was *really* dangerous. But you know, there was all that training. He just—it was okay."

This is something that Tom and Blake can appreciate, in a way. How one can be formed, disciplined—at times, in their own lives, they knew what it meant to push oneself, though it has been a long time since for both of them. To imagine the rewards David has achieved is to say to themselves that they could endure something difficult again, and that they would be similarly rewarded.

Tom goes to get another round of drinks and winds up talking to some girls—undergraduates, they must be. They look at him. They are at once given over to him. That is his power.

Perhaps they want to come drink with his buddies? "This is Blake. And this is Sam. Sam Katz."

"Oh," Sam says.

He can't really look these girls in the eye. It's hard. They're blond, tall, West Coast girls. They're from Malibu; they're from Laguna Beach or San Diego—nothing like Sam has seen before in his life. They didn't have these girls in New Haven. He's trying, Sam is; he *feels* close, but he's not there yet.

Tom and Blake are. They've done this a million times.

They order shots. "A round of GM!" Blake says. Sam peels off his jacket. He shows the girls a scar on his knee he got when he was in high school gym. He got caught up on the rusty winch of a tennis net—he did the tourniquet himself. They think he's cute. They sit near him.

"Sam-wise," one of the girls says, "my grandmother just died and she gave me this money. You could probably help me. You see, the thing, Sam-o, is this—"

Blake gets another call from his fiancée. He's got to go. Tom leaves, too. "Make sure that our friend gets home, okay?" Tom asks one of the girls. "Take care of our man Sam."

Over the course of the next month or two, pictures are shared. They no longer meet to study. Or rather, they meet to study David. It becomes, for Tom and Blake, a kind of nourishment. They need to believe in David, and if not David, the *idea* of David, for, as Tom himself would admit, a life without heroes is no life at all.

These photographs are only half-explained, and that is okay. Some are from business school trips that David has taken. Others are older, from when David was in the army. Some are from work trips—really, Sam explains, the firm for which he works is so diversified that they have investments all over the world.

A picture of a half-naked Muslim girl, hijab hanging from a burnished bedpost, panties pulled up into the cleft of her bottom, which is patterned with goose bumps, the half circle of one dark, small nipple exposed, the pillow beside her, where David lay, still crushed, still smelling of him—the smell of a young man's cologne, lavender and sandalwood. Her arm out to cover the lens, but they can see her giggling, her belly tightened.

A picture of a man—David, of course, yes, definitely—reclining in a plush chair in the lobby of the Oberoi. In this one, his hair is thick-cropped. "Well, it's old, the photo. This was before—" Sam says.

On that trip, he had a stop in Istanbul—the *real* Europe, Sam proclaims. He hooked up with a DEA friend there. Now, Sam says, *that* was a trip. "David says Turkish women are the most beautiful in the world. Even prettier than Czech women, who *everyone* says are the most beautiful. They're professional fellatrices."

"Professional *what*?" Tom asks.

Sam gestures. They get it, but watching him do it embarrasses them. Still, they're somewhat transfixed by Sam.

"They've perfected it over two thousand years. Since antiquity. It was a mark of a sophisticated woman in Byzantium."

A picture taken, lying down, of the domes of the Hagia Sophia. A man's hand obscuring the viewfinder at Pamukkale, the white terraces filled with boiling water. A picture of a man standing before Uçhisar Castle, at Cappadocia.

Tom holds the photo up—they are in the back of a bar—it's not bright enough. Blake takes the picture from Tom and they try to figure out how to get the best light. They can't see his face. Really, there aren't many of him.

"Well," Tom says, "I mean, who the hell takes pictures of themselves anyhow?"

"My fiancée," Blake says. "Brother. She's got to be in every shot."

"He's *got* to come out here," Tom says. "I mean, if you can't have fun here, then where can you? We should really meet him," Tom says. "Do you think he can make it?"

"Maybe," Sam says. "I'll ask him." His attention has turned to a woman. She is sitting at the bar; she looks like someone's mom.

Sam decides that he's going to talk to her. For Tom and Blake, such a thing wouldn't be so strange, but they're a little surprised at Sam. He leaves the pictures on the bar table. They think this one, in which David is looking away from the camera, would have been after a split with a longtime girlfriend. Here, the hotel lounge David goes to after a series of daylong meetings in Paris—the coal-colored bar, the glass, him laughing. This one, well, a girl he met, part of Javier Solana's group—did she have any career advice for him? They are trying to decipher an order, though they acknowledge that no order can be achieved.

"Listen!" they hear the woman from the bar say.

"I just—" Sam says.

There is a man—he's nearly sixty—talking to Sam. He's not happy.

"Young man—" the guy says.

Tom and Blake have to go over there. They have to make peace. *He's loaded*, they explain, *our man Sam is just totally wiped out. Give him a break, will ya?*

The man (it turns out that he's the woman's husband—if they'd been paying attention, they might have told Sam this) lets it slide. If he hadn't, Sam would've had Blake and Tom there to protect him, which they could have.

They leave. It's quiet. Driving to drop Sam off, they mention that they're planning a beach weekend. Maybe Sam wants to come?

"Sure," he says.

"And tell David that he's invited too, okay?" Tom says, chuckling.

This is during spring break. One of the other guys that Blake and Tom play club soccer with invites them to his folks' place. It's a large home on the water. They—at this point it's Blake and his fiancée, and Tom and this new girl he's seeing, Kristin—pick Sam up. He's sitting on the curb, waiting. He's got wide sunglasses on. He's wearing tight khaki shorts and a faded navy polo shirt. He's carrying a backpack. There is a water bottle nestled inside it.

"So that's him?" Laura asks.

"That's Sammy," Blake says. "His brother doesn't really look like him."

"Right. His brother is the spy?" Laura says.

Tom and Blake look at each other.

"Maybe it's best if you don't say anything to him about it," Tom says. "He can be a little dodgy about the whole thing. You'll like him. He's just a sweet—he's a nice guy."

Sam gets in the car.

"Hi," he says quietly.

Tom introduces him to everyone and especially his new girlfriend, Kristin.

"Sam," Tom says, "Kristin actually has a brother who works on Wall Street. He also went to HBS. I thought he might know your brother."

Kristin is sitting next to Sam. Her shorts are pulled up, her legs brown and smooth. Sam tries to make space, tries not to make contact with her, though it's hard, because Tom's legs, which are long, are spread wide, pushing her into Sam.

"Now, which firm is your brother with?" she asks.

"Oh, it's small. You probably wouldn't know it."

"My brother—Paul—he was with Blackrock. Have you heard of them? I mean, I'm sure you have. But he got out of it. He's a teacher now."

She's polite. She wants to speak with him. She is interested in Tom, whom everyone adores. A quality in him which is abundant and which she feels the need to examine, possibly extract. She still wants to make a good impression—though there is the sense that she won't always work for it, something Tom himself cannot see.

"What year was your brother in Cambridge?" she asks.

"He was there—well, it took him a little longer to finish, because the firm he worked with kept him on after his summer internship. So, it was a little more than three years, actually."

"Oh," she says, "So, when?"

Sam looks up.

"Um. Let's see. Two thousand and—wait, no. I think it was—"

Suddenly, Blake swerves the car. "Motherfucker!" he says. "Holy fucking shit! Did you see that asshole?"

He pulls up beside the driver in front of them, rolling down the passenger-side window. It's an old woman—she must be eighty—driving a Chevrolet Caprice.

"Lady!" Blake yells across Laura. "Will you get the fuck off the road!"

The old woman doesn't look at him.

"Now that's a shame," Sam says. "They should have mandatory age limits. Jesus."

At the house, there are a number of other couples. Blake and Tom—their shirts are off, their shoulders wide, hips lean—they drink endlessly. This has been a life for Tom and Blake; the better part of their education has consisted of just this.

Sam tries, too, but he quickly loses hold. He falls over things; he giggles; he must sit down. The girls, they lie about in bikinis on deck chairs. It is not something that Sam has seen before.

I can see him: Sam—his shirt off, pale, a runnel of hair down the middle of his chest. The other people don't know what to make of him. He goes in the water. He puts on snorkels. He talks to a girl named Caroline. Did she know he used to be on the swim team at his neighborhood pool? He shows her how he did the butterfly and he splashes great white waves, and she laughs.

"Where did you get this guy?" she asks. "He's something else."

In the late afternoon, Sam is lying down, passed out. Tom says that looking at him, they could imagine David—David as a superior version of Sam. David in the water of Kuşadasi. His body was brutal, the figure of one of those extreme fighters—cartilage formed over bone and joint. His face easy, his eyes deep, knowledgeable. He's not big—compact. He has such a strong heart. It is layered with pages of a story written by his little brother.

Sundown. They have barbecued. Sam is red.

"Sam-o," Tom says. "When is David coming out here? I mean,

really, could you pass up something like this? You gotta get him out here. It's craziness."

"I know, I know," Sam says. "I just talked to him last night. He's having a hard time."

"With what?" Tom asks. Everyone is now listening.

"He's sick of New York. The market is—well, the market. And it's getting old. But he doesn't want to go back to Washington. He can't stand it there. He's talking with an old West Point buddy. He may just travel for a time."

"I'm jealous," Laura says. "I'd like to meet your brother. I've heard a lot about him. I should ask him for some tips for Kenya."

Blake looks at her.

"Yeah?" Sam says.

"Now, Sam, you're from where? New York?"

"Laura," Blake says.

"That's what you told me," she says to Blake.

"Yeah. Well, the suburbs," Sam says. "Not the city. David lives in the city."

"Where?"

"Murray Hill," he says. "He's got a condo there."

"Nice," she says.

"Yeah. Hey, Tom," Sam says. "Did you say if you got that thing for the summer? At that firm?"

"Hold on," Laura says. "Can we just call him? I want to talk to him. I'm dying to get some *real* info. This one," she says, hitting Blake on the arm, "isn't the best when it comes to research. I'll give him a ring."

"I don't think—maybe not," Sam says.

She finishes her drink and pours another.

"Well," she says, standing. She is in a thin green bikini. It's night. "I want to talk to him. Is he coming out here? I can convince him," she says. "I'm confident. It'll be so fun."

Sam looks at Tom and Blake. Their faces are dark. They are not saying stop. It's beyond that now.

"It's too late. It's"—he looks at his watch—"it's almost midnight there," he says. "Maybe we can try him in the morning. I think I'm going to pack it in."

"Why not now?" she says. "I mean, maybe part of his sabbatical can be to come out here. Does he have something against the West Coast?"

"No," Sam says.

"What's his number?" she asks. "I'll call him. It'll be funny. Let me see your phone."

"It's—" Sam begins. He looks at Blake and Tom. His arms are crossed. He is in a T-shirt too big for him. He is pressed against the back of the chair. He adjusts his glasses.

"I'm beat. I really am," he says, and he gets up to go to his room. Tom and Blake let him go. Laura walks over to the pool.

"See," she says, and dives in.

"Wait," says Kristin, "I don't understand."

Tom gets up from the bar stool. He puts on his coat, huge, like a cape. The lobby is glowing; it's as if we are drowning in this aureate light. Outside, it's black and freezing, but Michigan Avenue seems to burn.

"You're right," I say. "I would have remembered. That's— I just—"

"Yeah," he says. "Right? Look, I don't want to give you the wrong idea. Sam really was a good guy."

He turns right and then left, stretching, as if he's wringing out his torso. He exhales. He pulls out from his pocket a money clip— cheap, but etched with his initials.

"This is what Sam got us," he says, showing it to me. It's fat with bills. He begins to unfold them, but I say no.

"You know, there's a time when you can see yourself in the future—you see *this*," he says, pointing to the bar. "You see yourself as the person you're going to be for a long time. Maybe the person you're going to be forever. And it's scary. It's like—I don't know. We just wanted to have a little fun. Maybe Sam, too. Do you think that's so strange?" he says bashfully.

"No. I don't think so. Not at all."

Tom puts his hand to his brow.

"I'm glad you were able to meet," he says. "Really."

"Please," I say. "I'm glad you thought to call me, Tom."

He walks toward the revolving door, where a woman in a long black coat, black cocktail dress, and black heels has entered. Her hair is dark, her face soft and very pretty. Tom looks her up and down as he leaves. She seems hurt, somehow, by the noise.

This woman walks over to the bellman. The sound of her heels knocking in the lobby—it's a kind of supremacy. He leans into her, saying something, and then he looks at me.

She walks away from him and stands near the staircase. Above, the rooms. She reaches into her purse, though she doesn't take anything out. She is waiting. I leave a fifty on the bar. I get up.

"Hello. Your name, sir?" the bellman asks.

"David."

LA JOLLA

To TELL ABOUT the two women: They met in a Spanish class; they had been paired up. The instructor said, "Lillian, ask Amy: *¿Con qué frecuencia vas al supermercado? ¿Una semana?*' Ask her: *¿Con qué frecuencia vas al dentista? ¿Dos años?*'" They laughed. At the end, Lillian asked Amy if she wanted to get a drink. They did, in Del Mar.

They looked alike. The ghost white blond hair and dark skin. And their bodies. Tall and lean—they were both runners. Lillian was fifty-eight that year, though she looked at least ten years younger. Amy was twenty-seven. It turned out they had gone to the same college, though Lillian said, "God, you weren't even *alive* when I was there!" They talked about the buildings and the dorms and what it looked like; they talked about the professors, though not for long— the ones Lillian had had were retired or dead by the time Amy got there.

They each had two martinis. Lillian had recently retired. Well, *retired* was not really the right word. She had closed a costume-jewelry store she ran with another woman. It was just a small business. Her husband, Marty, was a specialist at Scripps—a cardiothoracic surgeon. But he had cut back significantly. Finally, they had time. Was Amy married?

Yes. Her husband, Josh, was the reason they had come to San Diego. After finishing law school at NYU, he took a job at Fish & Richardson. Amy was still looking for work. Her master's degree had been in art history. Lillian said she had been in New York for the marathon last year, actually. She asked Amy if she'd been to certain restaurants, ones that Amy had only heard of.

The bartender wanted to know if they were sisters. He wasn't joking. Brown skin tight across their chests, the arms of volleyball players. Lillian with a diamond tennis bracelet, though it was real. The money—you could see it off her. Amy didn't have any friends yet, and neither did Josh. They had each other, but he worked a great deal. She wasn't worried.

"We'll take you kids out for dinner," Lillian said. "And we *have* to run together." Her running partner, Elaine, had had hip surgery. "We'll do the route up Torrey Pines. It's not hard at all. It'll be easy for you, but it's a good run for me."

Lillian insisted she pay—she would take no money from Amy. It was sixty dollars for the four drinks.

At home, Amy told Josh.

"How was class?" he asked.

"Good," she said. "I made a friend."

"Who is he?"

"Funny. It's a woman. Lillian. I think she's one of those wealthy country clubbers. She wants to meet you. Us. For dinner. She went to Smith, too. She runs."

"Yeah?" he asked. "That's good. Now you have a running partner."

"You're my running partner," she said.

They were sitting at the table. The furniture still smelled new, like laminate and stain—blond wood; curtains just hung. They had bought them with his signing bonus. They had been in San Diego for two months and Josh had put on ten pounds. He would take it off. He had played two years of football at Columbia, started his sophomore year but then quit.

"Do you care what night? I'm going to call her."

"No," he said.

"Okay, I'll call her. How was work?"

He smiled at her. She went over to him.

"Are you okay?" he asked.

"Yeah. I was glad to meet her. She's funny."

"I saw something for you," he said. "This." It was an advertisement for a job at an art gallery in La Jolla—a receptionist. "It's not much, but it might be something. Just until you get something more—you know."

"Oh," she said. "That was good of you. Okay. I'll call them."

"Whatever," he said. "It's just a lead. Take it or leave it."

She called Lillian the next day. Maybe she would want to run in the afternoon?

"Oh, baby, I already worked out." Then she was quiet, thoughtful. "Okay, why not? We'll do a short run, how about? Nothing major."

"No, no, that's okay," Amy said.

"No, really," Lillian said. "I want to."

"Are you sure?" Amy asked. She could hear the ocean through the phone. She could imagine the house. The deck overlooking the water. Maybe for her, in ten or twenty years, but probably never.

"Of course. Yes. Why don't we meet at the park at three?"

Lillian looked like that woman—the oldest Olympic swimmer. Only prettier. Her shoes were white and thick, and she wore ankle-cut Thorlos socks. Her legs were perfectly smooth and dark. She had on blue running shorts, a loose white runner's shirt. This time, she wore a thin gold anklet.

They hugged.

"Are you ready to do this?" Lillian asked.

The run was as hard as any Amy had ever done. Lillian did three miles before Amy could see any sweat on her. It was only her youth that allowed her to keep pace. They did that three to the top of Torrey Pines and then Lillian turned around and they did two back down. Amy could hardly keep up, and after, Lillian thanked her for getting her out again.

"You know that feeling when you have a little bit left from earlier? My morning thing just wasn't enough today. This was so great."

She could see that Amy was winded, and she was glad, though she watched her carefully. It took Amy only a couple minutes to catch her breath. Soon, the sweat dried around her hairline—a very thin white salted layer formed. Amy stood upright again, her breathing confident.

"I know it's not much for you," Lillian said. "It was probably easy. But it was a good thing *I* did it," she said.

"No," Amy said, laughing a little, "it was pretty much enough."

Lillian didn't believe her. Amy was thirty years younger and Lillian knew it'd take her a week to get back into her old form, maybe less. Amy's cheeks were lit from the sun. Her hands smooth, unlined. In two weeks, she'd murder Lillian. She'd be able to lap her.

They walked back alongside the ocean. Fog had come in and they couldn't see the shops above them. A man—he looked like a naval officer—with sloped shoulders and lean face was walking his dog. He stopped to ask them if they knew if the hilltop was fogged in, too.

"Not when we were there," Amy said. "Maybe now. Cute dog," she said, bending down to pet it.

He had asked Amy. It was obvious why. That's okay, Lillian thought. Walking next to Amy, the air smelled clean—like chlorine. Though they couldn't see it, gulls were landing on the stone border.

"Do you know a gallery on Herschel?" Amy asked Lillian. She gave the name. "I'm thinking of getting some work there. Just something part-time."

"Sure, I know it. They have some nice things. It's modern, right?"

"Yeah," Amy said. "I don't know. I figure it could be something for now."

"Did you ask Josh if he could make Saturday? Marty is eager to meet him. I can make us a reservation tonight. There's this great new place in Cardiff-by-the-Sea. You guys would love it."

Lillian's voice seemed to come from nowhere.

"Yeah," Amy said. "We're game."

Marty looked and had the swagger of a Dan Marino, only he hadn't let himself go. Josh pointed this out to Amy when Lillian and Marty arrived at the restaurant.

"Are you fucking kidding me?" Josh whispered. "How old did you say they were?"

"I don't know exactly. Our parents' age, I think," she said.

Together, they looked like a couple out of a catalog, only there was nothing dandyish about Marty. He had the same lean, drawn, but vital look as Lillian.

"You said this guy's a doctor?"

"A surgeon," Amy said. "A heart surgeon."

"How could his hands even *fit*?"

They talked first about the class Lillian and Amy were taking, and a bit about how they were both liking San Diego. But shortly after they'd ordered drinks, the conversation split, and Marty started to ask Josh questions. He was particularly interested when Josh mentioned that he'd played football, for he himself had played for a time at Yale, quitting after his freshman year—a torn rotator cuff.

"Now, of course, I'm talking *ages* ago. This was back when the Ivy League was just a bunch of guys who went to school and happened to be big enough to play football. You didn't need to be any good."

Marty asked Josh how long he had played, why he'd quit, which teams were now the best, what he had studied as an undergrad.

"How was Columbia when *you* were there?" Josh asked. "When you played them, I mean."

"Good. They were strong." Marty said, though Josh couldn't tell if he was lying. "A fine school."

"I guess we're like Yale, in a way," Josh said, "a good neighbor in a bad neighborhood."

Marty smiled.

"I had a son who went there, so we know it well," Marty said as he ordered them another drink.

Josh wasn't sure what this meant—*had* a son? Like, their son went there, or they no longer had the son? He didn't want to ask more.

Marty was soft-spoken, possessing the quietude of a man very aware of his own power, his success. He seemed in possession of, or capable of, great anger, possibly rage, even. Josh didn't know why he felt that way, but he knew many lawyers like that. Still, Josh liked him—it was hardly possible not to. The food came.

"You're a surgeon?" Josh asked.

"Yeah," Marty said casually. "Well, not much anymore, really. I mainly teach now. I've cut back significantly," he said. "In truth, I spend a lot of time now day-trading. It's really just for fun."

"Yeah, until you lose all our money," Lillian said, looking at Josh and Amy, though it was obvious such a thing would never happen. Like all accomplished men, Marty spoke of the market casually, as if it wasn't worth his full attention, just entertainment. Like golf or tennis, both of which he played as much as he could. Everything Marty said to Josh seemed as if it were a grave secret, to which only Josh would be privy.

The waitress asked if anyone wanted dessert. Amy and Josh shook their heads.

"Of course," Lillian said. "We'll all share." Everything was twenty dollars. Lillian ordered three things, then didn't eat any. The kids ate.

Mostly, they laughed. They had a fine time. Their first friends in town. They were the couple that Amy and Josh might be someday, but could only hope, and were now so far from it. There was an invitation for dinner over at the house—Marty had a range as big as a submarine and it rarely got used.

"Well, I'll tell you what," Marty said. "When we have you guys over, we can toss a ball around. We can air it out."

"You bet," Josh said, though he was a little drunk, and wasn't sure if Marty was kidding. But he wasn't. He wanted to see what

Josh could do. Josh, Marty saw, had the confidence of a young man who had been quite good once, and only needed to be let on the field to be good again.

"I'll get a new ball—what's your favorite?"

"Favorite what?" Josh asked.

"Football. I mean, Wilson, Spalding—what?"

Josh giggled. "Any," he said. "The kind with air in it." He felt good. It was the weather, he thought, the clarity of the light—one didn't experience this on the East Coast.

Marty laughed. "Good. We're on. You'll kill me, but it'll be fun." He wanted to test Josh out. See if he was really what he seemed.

Amy started work at the gallery at the front desk, though it was clear she would do very little. The owner, a Persian man named Hafiz, said that there was a possibility for promotion—she could even curate part-time if everything worked out. He was pleasant enough. He said there would be a lot of downtime. She could do her Spanish homework if she wanted.

That first week, Lillian came in.

"Hey there," Amy said, seated at a small desk near the front. Lillian waved her down.

"I'm looking for something for my home. We're renovating," she said loudly to Amy, so that Hafiz, whom she could not see but knew to be there, could hear her. She winked at Amy. "Can you please make some recommendations?"

Amy smiled. It was sweet, this gesture.

That day, upon Amy's recommendation, Lillian bought an eight-thousand-dollar print of the water by San Diego Bay. Hafiz told Amy that in the future she could earn a commission on a sale. Two days later, after the picture was hung, Lillian came back in with Marty in the late afternoon, she introduced Marty to Amy, acting again as if they didn't already know each other.

"This is my husband," she said. He smiled—teeth remarkably white. A chunky silver watch encircled his wrist.

That day, they spent $15,000 on a large iron sculpture and then came back the next day and spent $33,000 on a giant two-piece painting of a seagull that Amy showed them. When they went running the following week, Lillian said it was nothing at all. They were glad to help, and in any event, it all looked beautiful.

They did the same circuit and Lillian noted how this time Amy kept pace with her, as she'd expected, and even strode ahead on the back end by the beach. She lagged a step or two behind Amy, enjoying her smell. It was sunny this time, and she admired Amy's posture, the way the sun seemed to brown her shoulders even in the short distance they walked. The area around her eyes still soft, her elbows firm, clean. Once.

When they were finished, she said that Amy was a real sport for running with her.

"Here I am this old lady, and you're working out with *me*!"

"What? Lillian, you kick my ass. C'mon. And about last week. I don't know what to say. I mean, you two are amazing."

"Stop," Lillian said. They were crouched down in the grass, stretching, and Lillian lifted one hand. "Can you two come over this weekend? Marty is so excited to use his barbecue. He's been going to a specialty fish market. It's hilarious."

"Yeah," Amy said, though when she mentioned it to Josh later, he hesitated.

"We don't have to," Amy said, "but they spent a fortune last week and they seem excited. It's not like we have much else going on."

"No, you're right," Josh said. Which was true. And he did like Marty. And Josh felt guilty. There had been a position out of school at a very small firm in Boston, where Amy knew people, but Josh had much preferred San Diego. The weather was one thing. The other was the money.

The home. In La Jolla, up against the ocean. Wide and low, clean, sweeping lines from the road—one couldn't see how large it really was from the narrow street, but as they walked up to it, they could see straight through the foyer, where there stood a giant seven-foot-high circular aquarium; beyond that was the living room, and then the deck, a large French limestone patio and pool, which in the early evening was caught full up of the sun. Beyond that, the ocean.

"How much?" was what Josh whispered. "Don't even tell me less than fifteen," he said.

"Jesus," Amy said. The yard in front of the home was filled with melaleuca trees, specially planted, Lillian explained upon greeting them. It made everything seem cozy, though as Lillian walked them through the home, it was clear that it only *seemed* cozy. In many ways, they both thought the house was cold. The lines of the place arched, and though the cantilevered fireplace was in use, and the trees in the back were lush and in bloom, the home was missing something.

There were no photographs—not of Lillian and Marty, nor of children or family. The books filling the glass bookshelf in the library appeared unread, their spines shiny and clean, still in the dust jackets, all of them. They were the titles one would expect. The kitchen was giant, with steel appliances and black granite, and there were no pictures, no magnets, no notepads advertising drugs, no pens or pencils on the countertop near the phone. There was a large arrangement of pink lilies in the middle of the table, but that was it. Even the vase was glass.

In the bedroom, Amy nearly slipped on the polished cherrywood floor. The print they had bought from Amy was hung and appeared as if it had been there for a long time. Only, Amy noticed, the vibrancy it'd had in the gallery had diminished.

"The A-team," Marty said when Lillian brought them out back. He was hidden, around the corner of the home, beside a strange sloping white wall that separated the backyard from the driveway. He wore a gray apron.

Everything was laid out: a platter upon which sat thick tuna steaks, vegetables resting in a marinade that he'd prepared, he explained, and was experimenting with, so they should forgive him if it was a little off.

"We're really glad that you guys could make it," he said.

"Us, too," said Josh.

"And don't think you're off the hook, pal," Marty said. On a chair near the pool, whose water caught the sun on small dimples, sat a brand-new football.

"We're going down to the beach, my young friend—we're going to air this out."

Josh smiled. He was wearing six-hundred-dollar Zegna shoes. He hadn't thrown a football in five years. "You sure?" he said.

"Oh, yes," Marty replied. "You just have to promise to go easy on me."

Lillian said she would make everyone drinks. An ancient recipe, she said, though she didn't explain who had given it to her or where it had come from or what its ingredients were. When they sipped their drinks, Josh and Amy, sitting on chairs on the deck, Marty standing beside the grill, hair remarkably thick and dark, the food sizzling on the iron, it was strong, had the taste of— "What is this?" Amy asked. "It tastes like—is there Cointreau in this?" She took another sip. "No," Josh said. "This is . . . you know what this is? I'll tell you."

"You won't guess," Lillian said. "Just drink."

"This is tasty," Amy said. "What *is* this?"

"You all set, buddy?" Marty asked. "We've got about twenty minutes." He was serious about throwing the ball around. The sun was nearly going down. Josh looked at Amy. She smiled. *Go*, she seemed to say.

"Sure. Yeah, let's do it."

On the beach, Josh felt as if he were in the islands, almost out of life. Marty's hand fit nearly around the entire football and he threw as confidently as Josh thought he would. The surf was up. Josh had taken off his shoes and set them on some rocks and rolled up his pants.

Marty wanted to know how work was going and Josh said it was tough. The work itself was totally different from what he had learned in law school, not to mention how much he had to bill. Marty considered the ball—it seemed as if he knew what Josh was describing, understood and was deeply sympathetic. And things with Amy? Things with Amy were good, Josh explained, though his being out of the apartment all the time wasn't easy. Which was why it was good they had friends now. He was drunk, he realized, from the one drink Lillian had made.

"And what you guys did for her at the gallery—that was something else."

"We were happy to do it. It was something we wanted to do."

Marty watched how Josh handled the ball. Well, it was clear enough he'd played. He had a full ownership of his body. You could hear the laces off his fingers. Josh, Marty knew, was the fugitive athlete, the one who had been able to trade it all away and had done so willingly, to excel and establish himself in some other, unrelated discipline, if only to prove that he could. Josh was big and hearty, but not fat. He was the catcher in Little League, the lithe defenseman; he could shed the weight in an instant and be a threat in any position. That was his gift.

Josh coiled and uncoiled as he threw. His shirt stayed tucked in. He received the ball when Marty threw as if a child had thrown it. His skin was dark and clear, his eyebrows thick, jaw wide, nose large but dignified. Marty had known this kind of kid—the kind who seemed as if he could tear apart a tackling dummy, then went out partying later. Balled everything that moved. Hair on his hands. The heart strong as a train.

Marty inquired about Josh's law school loans. It was expensive out here, and he remembered that when he had finished up medical school, he thought he'd be in debt for the rest of his life. Josh didn't know what to say, but he agreed. Yes, it was a concern. "But it's a concern for everyone, right? I mean, it's the usual thing."

"Well, listen, I wanted to share a tip from a friend of mine—we went to school together. Undergrad. Well, it's not really a *tip*. I thought you guys might want to get into some stock that Lillian and I are in. I know half the board personally. Out in Houston," he said, holding the ball. "A defense contractor. They build airplanes. Anyhow, I want to get you guys—well, you know."

"Oh, that's okay," Josh said. "It'll be all right. My dad sort of has us set up with different funds."

"Oh, this is different," Marty said quickly. He wasn't insulted.

"That's okay. You guys have really done too much as it is," Josh said.

"Forget it!" Marty said. He threw the ball. "It's a perverse thing we do in this country. We force the brightest among us to pay for the right to earn the education they need in order to perform. Forget it, Josh, we'll get you all squared away."

Josh didn't know what that meant and didn't know what to say. The water was coming up very close now and Josh finally said that maybe they should go back up; perhaps dinner was ready. Marty said yes, probably he was right. He let Josh walk up the old wood steps to the back gate of the yard. Under Josh's shirt, his shoulders were bunched, and his hands were clean.

The tuna steaks didn't taste much like anything. The vegetables had either been overcooked or needed more salt. The wine they drank, and it was surely expensive, somehow tasted too fruity. The flatware was ultramodern and hard to use. At times there were moments of silence among the four, though Marty and Lillian didn't seem concerned about it. They would ask often how everything was and Josh and Amy always said something superlative.

At home, Josh asked Amy if she'd talked to Lillian about children. Did they have any?

"I don't know," Amy said. She was in bed. Her chest was dark from the sun and the running. Her breasts lay out to the side.

"Weird," Josh said. He took off his shirt and placed it in a hamper. The cuffs of his slacks had sand on them, he noticed. "And another thing. Marty wanted to put us into some kind of fund or stock or something? It was strange."

"It'd probably be good," Amy said, turning to him. "I mean, could you believe that house?"

"Yeah," he said.

"Was it fun throwing the football with him?" she asked. She was laughing a bit.

"It was okay. He wasn't bad. Actually, he was good. Still has it."

"I guess you never lose it," she said, moving closer to him.

That week, the four met up for tennis at Lillian and Marty's country club, where they had dinner afterward. They also met up for dinner, which Marty had arranged to pay for in advance, at an expensive restaurant owned by a famous TV chef. They went to a movie together.

Lillian remarked to them all how Amy was doing so much better in Spanish class. She would say how Amy was kicking her ass in their runs. Most of all, they would ask, ask.

Were they comfortable? Were they going back east for the holiday? Marty noticed that Josh had favored his left side on the tennis court. If he needed, Marty could get him in to see an osteopath right away. "No, really, I'm okay," Josh said. "Really? Because it's no problem. Don't even think twice about it. I know the best osteopath in the state," Marty said. It wasn't until he went to open his cell phone that Josh insisted he was perfectly fine, and had to tell Marty to put his phone away.

They were being scrutinized. Surveilled. At times, Lillian and Marty didn't speak, but were caught just looking at Amy and Josh, who would always say something banal, just to break the silence. What was it? they would ask later at home. What did these people want? They felt as if they were being classified, categorized. It was something physical. Josh didn't like it. Amy, who was very pretty, was used to it, in a way, but said that, yes, it was strange.

They received a letter from a broker in New York, who explained that a large number of stock shares had been purchased in their names as a gift. They didn't need to ask who'd given these to them. Josh called up Marty at the hospital.

"Dr. Childress's office," a young woman said.

"May I speak to Dr. Childress, please?"

"May I ask who's calling?"

"My name is Josh Mullen." He added, "I'm an attorney."

There were a few moments of silence and then Marty came on the phone.

"Hey there, pal."

Josh could imagine Marty at his office, the plain wide desk before him, certificates and degrees over his shoulder, all from the best schools.

"Marty, we got a letter that you and Lillian bought us some stock?"

"Oh, that," he said. "Good, I'm glad it arrived."

"Well, I'm sorry Marty, but we can't—" Josh didn't even finish before Marty interrupted him.

"Listen pal," Marty said. "It's not a question of 'can't accept' or 'can.' We just wanted to do this for you. These years," he said, referring to Josh's and Amy's, "are really hard. We've been there. We just want you not to worry. We worried for a long time, and we don't want you guys to have to."

"Still," Josh said, "I'm just not sure I'm comfortable with the whole thing, Marty. I mean, it's really very generous of you guys, but we simply can't accept it. It's just too much."

For a few seconds, Marty didn't say anything. Josh felt his throat tighten, and his back began to sweat. This was the part of him that was growing—the lawyer. He felt it was good, an armor that he needed to build up.

"Hmm," Marty said, and then there was a tone on Marty's end of the phone, and Marty said, "Oh listen, pal, I've got to go. Listen, we'll talk about this next time, okay? On the courts, man. Get your serve warm," and then he hung up.

During the next few weeks, Lillian and Amy continued to see each other at their Spanish class, and they continued to run together, but all four of them did not gather. They'd stretched out their run by three miles, and it was clear to Lillian, as it had been on their first run, that it was just a matter of time before Amy returned to her old form.

Amy ran with her shoulders back, her stride long and confident, and though one would not be able to say from a distance who was the elder, who was better, Lillian could tell. To her, it was obvious. Amy didn't say anything about the stock.

That matter was more difficult. The man at the brokerage firm who handled the account said he could indeed return the money to Marty, but he was a little unclear. He said it was his impression that the shares were simply remuneration for services rendered by Josh and Amy, a payment given in the form of a gift to avoid taxes. Josh said no. He said he didn't understand.

"Well," the man said, "what would you like me to do?"

Josh held off and then held off some more. There was the issue of pride, but there was also the issue of indebtedness.

"Sure," he said, "the guy gives us a gift, but it has strings attached."

"Maybe not," Amy said, though she felt, too, that it might.

In any event, they figured that if Marty and Lillian could drop that kind of cash so easily, then what would really be the harm in accepting it? It simply didn't mean anything to them.

So, the following week, when Lillian phoned and suggested they all get together for a round of golf, Amy said they couldn't, and made sure not to give a reason why. "Oh," Lillian said quietly. "Okay." And when she called again to see if they wanted to meet at the country club for drinks and dinner, they declined. "Okay," Lillian said. "I understand."

"Lillian—" Amy began, but she didn't finish.

"It's okay," Lillian said.

When an art gallery opened downtown, Lillian called Amy, but Amy said they already had plans, which wasn't true.

Amy *was* working and doing well at the gallery. Josh had been invited over to a friend of a friend's place for a card game, a guy named Tom, who was also new to San Diego. Josh was excited about it, and it turned out to be a lot of fun. Soon, the Spanish class ended, and soon they no longer received any calls from Lillian and Marty. They had done nothing with the money except leave it be. The women still ran together, only it was just that—running partners. Lillian would purposefully let Amy get ahead, standing a bit behind.

Eventually, Amy e-mailed Lillian to say she'd hurt her ankle and she'd be out for a bit.

"How long?" Lillian asked. "Because Marty can get you in to see someone right away."

But Amy didn't write back.

A couple of months later, in the fall, Amy discovered that a charity event, an event that Tom and his girlfriend, Kristen, had helped organize, which supported increased research into infant mortality, fell on the same weekend as a wedding they had to attend in New York. They had already bought tickets at $250 apiece.

"We can't waste them," Josh said.

"Maybe we can give them to Lillian and Marty," Amy said.

They were on their way out for a run after work. They ran together now at least twice during the week, and every day on the weekend. Josh ran with his shirt off.

"Yeah, we could," he said.

"I think it would be nice," she said. "I think it would be appropriate."

"Yeah," he said. "Okay. Why don't you call them?"

She did. Lillian said they'd be delighted to go. And then she added that it was very kind of Amy and Josh to offer. Amy said she'd drop the tickets off, and she did, leaving them in the mailbox.

No one at the event knew who Marty and Lillian were. Mainly, it was young couples. It was held in the ballroom of the Del Coronado. Pink, yellow, and light blue banners draping the walls, pictures of healthy round babies blown up to giant sizes, faces smiling.

There was a couple at the door who greeted Marty and Lillian.

"Hi!" the young woman said.

"Hello," Marty said, and handed her the tickets.

She looked down at the table, where small laminated paper bottles with the attendees' names and table numbers on them were spread out.

"Josh and Amy Mullen?"

They smiled.

"Here you go," she said.

"Thank you," Marty said.

They talked with the people at the table. There was a woman sitting near Lillian, an assistant professor of Latin American literature at UCSD. Lillian told her that she'd been taking a Spanish class and said she'd started on her own to read Cortázar.

"Not bad," the woman said. "You are on your way."

Marty was sitting near a young man who had started his own architectural landscaping firm, and Marty told him that their house had actually been featured in *Architectural Digest* because of the pocket garden they'd built beside their bedroom.

"It's really something," Marty said.

"I'd love to see that," the young man said.

"We'll have you over some time," Marty said. "I'll give you the tour."

The young man asked a bit about Marty. He wasn't able to tell how old he was. But he seemed to be a good guy.

"Well, I'm a doc over at Scripps," he said. "But in truth, I've cut back significantly. Mainly, I teach now. And mess around day-trading," he said, smiling. Marty explained that he played tennis a few nights a week with his wife—here he gestured to Lillian—which, he said, was a departure from back in the old, old days, when he played football.

"You know," the young man said, "Tom—over there—he was some kind of athlete, too, I think. I think he played baseball for a time."

"Really?" Marty said.

There was an auction. The first item up for bid was a series of golf lessons with San Diego's top pro, which went for two thousand dollars. The next was a weekend trip to Napa Valley, a wine tour included, which a couple spent $7,500 on. There was a basketball game with a former L.A. Lakers player few people had heard of. There was a trip to Sundance. There was an all-expenses-paid race-car trip to Turin, Italy, which went for $25,000. The ballroom was humming. Marty and Lillian looked around at all the children. Wonderful.

The last item up for bid was actually a cottage in the Turks and Caicos. One of the chairs' parents was putting it up for auction. The opening bid was for two million dollars, and that was placed by the CEO of a dot-com. It was raised by a young man who'd inherited a fortune from his father, a timber tycoon. It was raised again by a young woman whose parents ran the largest liquor distributorship in North America. Lillian whispered something to Marty, who then raised it to $5.25 million. After that, no one else bid on the home and it was announced sold.

The crowd clapped; the young couples cheered. The young man, the landscaper, patted Marty on the shoulder.

"Josh, my friend, you are one cool customer. Jesus Christ."

"Well," Marty said. "It's for a good cause."

Later, Tom approached them. Lillian and Marty were standing by a window, their backs to the ballroom, looking out onto the ocean. They weren't speaking. Kristin watched from far away, her face sour and unsure.

"I'm sorry," Tom said. "Are you friends of Josh and Amy's?"

Lillian and Marty turned to face him.

For a few seconds, they were quiet. Lillian looked down briefly and reached out to Marty, who clasped her hand and seemed to squeeze it, as if reminding her of something. On her finger sat a diamond, its edges sharp. Around Marty's wrist was the silver watch, big and cold as a manacle. Lillian looked up. Standing straight, they smiled at Tom. Even in the dim light, their teeth gleamed.

"So," Marty said finally, "I understand you played college ball?"

A year later, Amy—she was pregnant with her first by then—was leaving the gallery, and she thought she saw Lillian. She was with a young woman who might have been her daughter, though, of course, Amy didn't know if Lillian had a daughter.

They were in a car, which was parked on the street. The woman Amy thought was Lillian sat on the passenger side of the long white convertible, her head down, looking at something. Her hands, Amy thought. She wore a wide hat that put most of her face in shadow, and she had on big dark sunglasses, which, Amy felt, for some reason, concealed old, sunken, yellowing eyes.

It was 2:00 P.M. and she was on her way to meet Josh. They were shopping for homes. He believed he was going to make partner within a couple years and there were the dividends from the stock Marty had given them, which had spiked, a portion of which they planned to use as a down payment.

Amy stood beside an SUV. She watched. The young woman closed the trunk of the car, seemed a bit breathless, as if she had hefted something into it, and walked to the driver's side and got in. The two sat in the car for a moment before the young woman started the engine.

It was unusually warm, and Amy put her hand out to the side of the SUV. She reached for her phone. She wanted very badly to call Josh. She would say to him that she thought she saw Lillian. Yes, right now. *Here,* across the street.

The car pulled out into the lane. No. It probably wasn't her. It couldn't be. The woman in the car rested her hand on the door, raised her head to the sun, took a deep breath. Amy walked out from behind the SUV and held on to the phone, pretending she was dialing. The car came along beside her slowly, and Amy turned away, ashamed.

FOR THE RECEPTION TO FOLLOW

THE GROOM'S SIDE flew in from Los Angeles, the bride's side from Kansas City. The night before the wedding, there had been a dinner at a country club. Toasts were given—the best by the groom's friend Tom, who said that he was a better guy for having been friends with the groom, the groom a better man for marrying the bride. Everyone clapped. When he returned to his seat, people watched him.

Later, back at the hotel, Tom stood near the bar. Ben came up beside him.

"Can I get a—" He wasn't sure what he wanted. He looked to see what Tom was drinking.

"How about a scotch and soda?" he told the bartender. Tom smiled. He wore a white shirt, dark slacks. He was tall. It looked as if he'd walked off the golf course.

"Mother's milk," Tom said, raising his glass just a little.

Ben looked at him.

"Cheers," he said to Tom. "Good job, by the way. Your buddy should be thankful."

"Oh," Tom said. "Well, he's a good guy."

"All you guys went to school together?"

"Oh, yeah. Forever ago," he said, which was silly. "We had a good time. Well, that's what everyone says. Whenever I tell anyone where I went to college, they say, 'I bet you had a good time.' How do you know them?"

"My girlfriend, Ellen. She worked with Abby at AOL."

"Out in D.C.?" Tom asked.

"Yeah. Well, close."

"That's funny," Tom said. "We're moving there, actually. My girlfriend is going to law school. I'm tagging along."

From the far end of the lounge, Ellen looked for Ben but couldn't find him. He wasn't with the people they'd been seated near at dinner, the only people he knew, though, of course, he didn't know them well.

Ellen looked for Ben in the lobby. She became worried. Had he gone back to the room? She was about to go upstairs to find him, when he was revealed as Tom turned to face away from the bar. Ben was standing next to Tom, grinning. Tom, whom at least two women had asked Ellen about after his toast. What was his story? I don't know, she'd said. I don't know anything about him.

That summer, upon Ben's recommendation, Tom and his girlfriend, Kristin, moved into the building in which Ben and Ellen lived. Ben and he had exchanged e-mails over the summer as Tom was finishing a consulting job in San Diego, and when a listing became available, Ben had notified Tom.

"That's so funny," Ellen said. "You meet this guy at the wedding, and her—what is she, his fiancée?"

"His girlfriend. Yeah. Isn't it? I mean, I kind of felt bad for them. They don't know anyone. I mean, they know me, I guess. But I didn't even really meet her at the party. We just talked for a bit. But he's a good guy. You'll see."

On the day they moved in, Tom came by to say hello. Ellen answered the door. Tom was wearing ancient loose cargo shorts, a gray T-shirt, under which Ellen could see the rise of his chest, running shoes that were worn near the outer edges, for he was the slightest bit bowlegged. He hadn't shaved in two days. He looked to her like one of those college track stars, and he was very handsome, it was true.

"Hi," he said. "I'm Tom."

"Oh, hi," she said. "I'm Ellen."

"I wanted to come by to thank you. Well, thank you and Ben. Is he around?"

"You know, he's not, actually. I mean, he *is,* but he's out for a second. He just went across the way to get something to drink."

"Oh," Tom said. He was disappointed. "So, you work over there at AOL?"

"Yeah," she said. "I'm a statistician there. That's how I knew Abby."

"Statistics?" Tom said, as if this were an exotic job.

"Yep. We're like doctors," she said. " 'Today we're feeling well. Last week, not as well.' "

He smiled.

"That's great. Well look, I hope you guys can come by later. We kind of wanted to thank Ben. Well, you and Ben."

"Yes. Great," Ellen said. "What floor are you on?"

For a second, Tom looked confused, and he stepped back so that Ellen could see that they were on the same floor; they were right across the hall.

She didn't even know that apartment had opened up—there had been two Orthodox Jews living there and a little baby. She thought the husband had been a lawyer. They hardly knew anyone on the floor—it was very quiet. There was an older woman, a widow, they suspected, with a dog, who lived at the end of the hall, but that was it.

"We're just over here. We'll try not to make a lot of noise. We'll be done soon. I just wanted to thank Ben for helping us. Kristin did, too."

"Oh. Okay. Well, we'll come over," Ellen said. "I guess when— well, when Ben gets back. So, I guess, welcome."

She closed the door. Through the peephole, she watched Tom walk into his apartment. It was three steps away. Close. He stood on the threshold. He looked around. He seemed to be talking to someone out of sight from Ellen, but she couldn't hear anything. And then he closed the door, too.

———

It was around seven that Ben and Ellen walked across the way. Ben had thought it would be a good idea to bring them something—a housewarming gift. They'd made brownies. Ben had wanted to help, which she thought was nice. He'd tried on three different shirts. When it was time to go, he'd walked away from his desk quickly, left a document open, in mid-sentence, which he never did—he was compulsive about finishing his work.

Kristin opened the door. Well, Ellen could see why Ben was nervous. Kristin was nearly as tall as Tom, tan, wide shoulders. She had long wavy black hair, which was held up by a red bandanna. Having moved across the country, boxes stacked neatly in place, Kristin didn't seem at all weary. She was graceful.

Somehow, Ben would have seen a picture of Kristin—perhaps Tom had sent it to him. In any event, Ellen wasn't worried.

On the table, there was a bottle of champagne.

"Well," Kristin said, "we'd had it forever. I hope it's cold. We'll see," she said.

Tom came out from the back, pulling on a fresh shirt—his belly stuck out the way that a bodybuilder's would.

"Hey!" he said, coming over to greet Ben and Ellen. He saw that they had brought brownies. "Oh, you guys!" he said, but it wasn't false. It wasn't the least bit false; it was as genuine a thing as either of them had heard.

Kristin was starting law school, though there was nothing of the lawyer about her. She mentioned something about wanting to work in the nonprofit community. She and Tom had met through friends, though neither explained which friends. Through a buddy from college, Tom had arranged a short-term consultancy with a government contractor, a project he'd be working on largely at home: reviewing a division's financials, culminating in a report. There was a possibility for coming on board permanently if all went well.

They asked about Ben and Ellen. Ellen explained everything:

that they'd met in graduate school (Tom and Kristin gave an indication of being impressed, which everyone did, when she said where). She'd been studying statistics and Ben had been doing his own Ph.D. in mathematics, though he'd quit.

"What do you do now?" Kristin asked Ben.

"I'm a futurist. Well, not really a futurist. But I'm a *writer* for a futurist"—a gig he got while in graduate school, working for a cultural anthropologist. Ben explained that he was paid by this futurist, who was employed by movie studios to predict what the future would look like.

"That's crazy," Tom said, laughing a little, as if he were trying to emphasize how crazy it was. "I told you," he said to Kristin. "Isn't that cool? That's something else."

"I don't get it," Kristin said. "I mean, I do, but I don't."

Ben explained that his boss would use him to write a proposal for a director or a screenwriter. They're hired as outside consultants. It was a great gig. He worked from home. Maybe twenty hours a week, but he was paid like a lawyer.

"So, what do we need to know?" Kristin asked. She sat next to Tom on the sofa. They did not touch.

"In the future," Ben explained, "the most powerful entity will be the International Olympic Committee. Nation-states, or at least the *idea* of them, will cease to exist. Sport will be the only common language. Citizens will be divided up not on the basis of race, but of sport. Revolutions will be efforts at recognition by the IOC."

The true heroes of the future, Ben explained, will be the athletes.

That night, they ate the brownies and drank champagne. They had the door to the balcony open. Kristin took Ellen in back so that she could show her how the place was going to shape up. Well, she would be busy with school, that was certain, but she wanted to decorate at least a little bit.

Tom and Ben sat in the living room. Ellen could not hear what they were saying.

———

Ben and Ellen talked about getting married; of course they talked about it. It had been two years. They were doing well. He had work for the next decade, with all those Marvel Comic adaptations. As a statistician, Ellen could work anywhere.

But there were certain little things. Really, they were *so* little, it was silly; it was hardly worth mentioning, and so they never did. When they ran together (which was infrequent) through the park, there was an area of skin on the back of her arms that quivered. She would often say that she had to lose about ten pounds, maybe fifteen. She said it all the time. He never agreed with her. What difference did it really make? In any event, she would fall behind him.

They had sex once a month, sometimes less—it seemed enough. Also, there were things she would never do, never even try. There were other things she *would* do, but only on birthdays and holidays— that was how she put it. *Birthdays and holidays,* which Ben didn't think was so great.

Ben was very quiet. His body—it was as if it had not changed since he was thirteen. His hips were bony, but it was clear they wouldn't be in ten years. They would widen like a tube. His hair—it was thinning at the crown and near the hairline. He didn't have long before his scalp would shine through altogether. His fingers and wrists—they joked about this—were thinner than hers.

It was a list that meant absolutely nothing if you were an adult, and if you were a serious person, and if you knew that no one was perfect, including yourself; if you had never been faced with some-one who was perfect.

On her birthday in September, Ellen came in from work. The doors to her apartment and Tom's were open. She heard Ben explaining something to Tom. She stood outside, listening.

"We don't really know who she is. I mean, she's probably the rich-est lady in the building, but all she does is walk this dog. Like, six times a day. She wears that floppy hat. She's strange, too. She won't look you in the eye."

"That's funny," Tom said, "I've seen her. I haven't gotten her name. She's goofy, though."

They were describing their down-the-hall neighbor, the old woman, the one every building has—the one who would let the police know if she saw a black man loitering.

Then, for a bit, they didn't say anything. It was silent. Ellen looked into Tom's apartment to see if Kristin was there, but she was not. All their things were in place, but Kristin had not decorated whatsoever. She saw a table, chairs, couch—no television.

She heard Tom say something like *I appreciate it.*

"Well," Ben said, "I mean, it can be hard. We came here together. And Washington is a very particular kind of place. So, I think I know—"

She walked into the apartment.

"Hey," she said.

Ben and Tom sat on the sofa, their legs up on the coffee table. They were in T-shirts that were soaking. Tom was looking out the window. Ben was looking at Tom's glass of water.

"Hey," Ben said.

"Hi," Tom said.

"Ben, I thought that we were going straight out for drinks?" Ellen said as she put her things down.

A look—it wasn't remembrance, but more like annoyance—came over him.

"Yeah. Yes. You're right. We just went for a run. I'll go—I'll shower real quick."

"Oh boy. I gotta go anyhow," Tom said, which bothered her. *Anyhow,* she thought. That wasn't right. He smiled at her. He went to put his glass in the sink.

"See ya," he said, and walked past Ellen. He smelled clean, despite the ribbon of sweat around his neck and down his back.

"I'll be out in a minute," Ben said, going in the back to shower.

At the dinner—it was a restaurant she had chosen and had made the reservations for—they sat very quietly. The waitress asked what Ben wanted to order, but he didn't respond to her, and Ellen had to say something to him. They talked, but only a bit about work. It was superficial. It didn't feel like a celebration.

Ben talked a little about Tom. He said that actually, they had been going to the coffee shop during the days to work. Well, Ben to work and Tom to sketch out the framework of his report. He needed Ben's help with it—he was having trouble organizing everything.

"So, you have a buddy," she said.

"Yeah, I guess. Well, it's nice during the day, at least," Ben said.

The lights of the restaurant were high, and they cast shadows over everything. Looking at her, he could see exactly how her face was going to begin to fall—her chin, her cheeks. She wore a sleeveless top. Her arms.

"You two went running?" Ellen asked. "You didn't remember that I told you we were going out right after work? You didn't remember that?" Which was surprising, for Ben remembered nearly everything.

"You know, Tom said that Kristin does this circuit—she runs and swims. You can swim here in the city for free, you know. I thought I'd mention it to you. It might really—well. I guess it's something to think about."

Ellen said some things. He tried to explain himself.

That night, no cake was brought out to Ellen. Ben had gotten her—she couldn't believe it—a series of gift cards to the bookstore and housewares stores. They left quietly. When they returned home, she looked to see if the light was on or sound was coming from Tom and Kristin's apartment. Ben did, too.

The following week, Ellen called Kristin at her apartment. Tom picked up the phone.

"Hi, Tom. It's Ellen. From across the way?"

"Oh, yeah. Hi. Hey. What's up?"

"I wanted to see if Kristin was around."

"You know, she's not. She's over at school."

"Oh, okay."

"How is everything over there? How is AOL feeling today?"

"Um," she said, "pretty good. We're feeling well today. We had a hiccup last week, but I think we're on the mend."

"You guys lost some people," Tom said, which Ellen was surprised that he knew.

"We did, but the doctors are safe. For now."

"Yep," he said. She could imagine him stretching out at his desk, the band of his shorts tight across the pan of muscle. "We need the doctors. We can't live without them."

"Well, thank you. It's true. This is what I keep telling my manager. Listen, Tom, I wanted to find out—Ben mentioned this to me—about this exercise thing that Kristin does. I'm trying to get back in it a little bit, and I thought Kristin—she works out a lot, right?"

"Oh, yeah. You bet."

"Well, I wanted to find out what exactly she does. I wouldn't do the same thing at first, of course, but maybe I could start light."

"Well, I mean, I could tell you. In fact, if you wanted, we could go together. To the pool. It's at the pool. I'm going there anyway. I can't look at this page any longer. I've been writing for an hour."

"Oh, no," Ellen said. "I'm so out of—I mean, I'd be like so slow."

"I'm going anyhow, Ellen," he said. This seemed genuine.

"Really?"

"Yeah. Do you know where it is? We can go after—what time do you get off work? We can meet there if you like."

"Okay," she said. "Sure."

Ellen came in at nine o'clock. Her hair was wet.

She went into the office, where Ben was working.

"Hey," she said.

"Hey. Where were you?" he asked.

"I took your advice. I went to work out. I went to the pool."

"Oh. With Kristin?"

"No. With Tom. He—I mean, he put me through the wringer. He really—you weren't kidding."

"What do you mean?"

She explained their workout. They were there for an hour and a half. He wouldn't quit. It was something else.

"I told you," Ben said.

She sat down on the small sofa. She took off the fleece she was wearing. Her things were to the side.

"I feel it already," she said. "Like, here," she said, rubbing her stomach and then her shoulders. Ben was quiet.

"Well, there you go. It's good," he said.

"I left before he did," she said. "He was going to stay another hour, I think. Did you know about this couple's triathlon thing they did when they were in San Diego?"

"He mentioned something. I think—yeah."

Ellen sat on the floor. She stretched out.

"I'm so hot. I'm, like, still sweating." She took off her shirt. All she had on was her bra. Ben came over. She smelled like chlorine.

He looked at her bag.

"Is your swimsuit in there?" he asked.

"Yeah," she said, confused.

He pulled it out and laid it on the sofa. He looked at it for a moment, then reached down behind her, and in a very quick motion, he unsnapped her bra.

"The rest," he said, and she did.

They did not discuss it; they did not collude. Kristin was always at law school. Tom would walk over quietly in the morning, see Ellen off to work, share a cup of coffee with Ben. He had his own place at the end of the large table, where he would sit as the light came up over the buildings across from them, and Ben could see him most clearly, perfectly resolute. Tom's smell in the morning—starchy, warm—this was a privilege.

The report was not going well. The manager had expressed some concerns. Tom had come so highly recommended but the work he had produced so far was muddled. How did Ben and Ellen do it? They were, like, geniuses.

"We'll fix you up, Tom. Don't you worry, pal," Ben would say.

They would go to a coffee shop. Ben would write—Tom envied this—so quickly. He'd write one perfect page in five minutes, as if it was all there in his head, simply to be typed. Tom struggled. Ben read his work—it was dreadful. It was the writing of a diligent but slow high schooler.

And there were the women. A day would not go by where one wouldn't find a reason to talk to Tom: Was there an outlet near him? Had she left a pen by his seat? He would speak to them as if he were speaking to an old, dear friend. He never seemed surprised, which Ben took to indicate a vast experience. Often, they would find a way to leave him their e-mail address. Then he would return to his work, dismayed, hopeless.

"You know what I find," Ben would say. "I think when you get writer's block, you need to set it aside. Like, we should get our minds off this stuff. Clear our heads a little bit."

"You're right," Tom would say. "You're really right, Ben. I appreciate it. I really do."

During the better part of the afternoon, Ben and Tom would go to the park. In the green, deep bowl between the zoo and the parkway, Tom would share his knowledge. That period was divisible by sets and repetitions, exercises that had colorful names but which destroyed the body. Ben repeated with difficulty what Tom did so easily. Watching them, one would think they were performing a kind of martial art—they did not speak, their movements were synchronous while Ben fell into what seemed like the ghost image of Tom, his own body unable to fill even the space just occupied. As the sun fell over the tree line, it was as if they were being spotlighted. Tom did these things with his shirt off. Drivers would slow down.

By early evening, and though Ellen said she had tried to contact Kristin, she would also meet with Tom. In the few hours away from Ben, he would need another break. They would meet at the pool. He would stay later.

"You go," he would say, standing on the deck, his drag shorts having been pulled tighter and tighter across his waist, certain muscle formations revealed, though not in a good way. He was growing lean. "I'm going to hang back," he'd say, looking at the pool. "I need to finish."

Kristin, it seemed, was a boarder in their apartment. They rarely spoke. She'd found a group of friends at law school. She had camped out up there. Once, Tom went out with them and they spent the entire time talking about a real estate precedent, and Tom watched baseball, recalled only to himself his former accomplishments. The people they met in the city were interested in things like where you went to school, whose office on the Hill you'd worked in. In Washington, people didn't *do* jobs; they worked *on* them. *You know Chris—he works* on *the Sudan. Ally works* on *gender inequality in India.* They discussed SIM cards and places they had traveled to—they reviewed the stamps in their passports as if they were medals. Like Tom, Kristin had never been out of the country and seemed enrapt. Though he could not see it, she was simply in the final stage of siphoning off his power.

Mostly, Tom would stay in. The apartment still smelled foreign to him. There were marks on the thresholds of all the doors where the people before him had hung some religious ornament—one they had even left behind accidentally—he didn't know what it meant but felt it was so personal, felt that it was haunting the place. In the office, he would look at his computer, stand over the window, look down at the street, where the strange old woman walked her dog. Often they would stop, she pointing at a new door or a truck, some important feature. Some time ago, he would have gone out to

a bar. It would be a drink, then a new friend, then—but he was trying to make a go of it with Kristin. At night, alone in bed, he'd
think that he could hear the old woman speaking to the dog from
down the hall.

He tried to think of what he had. His neighbors. Ben and Ellen.
They were close and very open. It was something to be thankful for.
That they were willing to spend time with him. They didn't judge
him. He knew his limitations. He started to sleep in, sometimes until
eleven or noon, would skip breakfast and lunch, and Ben would
come over.

"Hey, man," Tom would say. "I'm dying here. I need a break.
What do you say to going to get a coffee? Or if you want, we could
even skip it altogether and just go to the park?"

Often, Tom would think he was graced.

"You know—I think definitely. Let's get out of here," Ben would
say.

They'd leave. Tom would do what he could do very well.

Only, over winter break, Tom had informed them, somewhat hesi-
tatingly, that Kristin and he planned to hang out. They needed to
stop things for a bit. She had been so busy, they were going to—
well, they were just going to do nothing. They needed to reconnect,
he and she. In truth, things were not going very well between them.
Just after Thanksgiving, they all four had dinner. Tom and Kristin
hardly spoke to each other, and it was clear that Kristin didn't want
to be there.

"You know, Kristin," Ben said, "I read this article about how because the market is so bad these days, law students are taking, like,
anything. You know, just to get a foot in the door?"

"Oh," she said.

"Anyhow—and I don't know if this would be of interest to you,
but I have this buddy. I was talking to him. Real smart guy. He's
doing a case now and said they're working through the holidays and

needed people. I guess there's all these millions of pages of discovery. Anyhow, I could mention something to him, if you were interested. It could lead to something. You never know."

"You mean Steve?" Ellen asked, smiling.

"What?" Kristin asked. "What's so funny?"

"Nothing," Ellen said. "I know Steve. He's a good guy. A good guy to know. He's—well, he's terrific. He'd be good to apprentice under."

Tom looked at Kristin. His face—it was thinner. One could see the small, delicate bones around his eyes. Kristin looked at him.

"That's—yeah, I think that'd be sort of a coup," Ellen added.

Kristin had heard of the firm. It would be unlikely that she'd get a summer associate offer there without knowing someone, and they knew that one had to take advantage of every opportunity possible.

"Yeah," Tom said. "That would be great. Right?"

"Sure," Kristin said. "I mean, yes. That's really thoughtful of you to mention, Ben. I'd definitely like to."

Ben contacted his friend and Kristin started work immediately after her finals. It was a ton of hours, but they needed the money, and Tom could always use more time to write.

In January, there was a cold snap—the entire country was twenty degrees colder than normal—and so, because Tom had the time (Ellen ended up taking time off work), they spent the days in the pool.

In the water, Tom stood before them. The drag shorts around his waist were pulled so tight, the extra drawstring had to be wrapped over itself. His body, in the fluorescent light, was yellow. His shoulders were like softballs that had been peeled of their covering—one could see the joints, the bone under the muscle, the shifting of these things.

He would call out sprints for Ben and Ellen. They would compete. They were like children. Tom would swim with them, often looking out of the high windows. They had bought heavy inflatable rubber balls and would do lunges across the length of the pool. Mothers and their little children played at the other end.

"I think I won that last one there," Ben said. "What do you think, Tom? I murdered her."

"Bullshit," Ellen said. "If anything, it was a tie. Tom, set this guy straight. You need glasses, Ben. I'm not joking. I had you by a mile."

Tom floated in the deep end. He went under the water. He held on to the side of the pool, watching Ellen and Ben. He envied them. Their lives were ordered, accomplished.

In the locker room, changing, Ben said he had to run across the way to give Ellen something. He went into the women's locker room. There were two young girls at the far end. She was still in her bathing suit. She stood looking at the back of her calf, flexing it forward and back, admiring some new quality about it.

She saw Ben. She wasn't surprised. She took him by the hand and led him into the shower. She turned it on. He pulled the plastic curtain across. They could hear the two girls laughing as they threw their swimsuits into the machine to dry them. Ellen started to take down her suit, but Ben stopped her. Looming over her, he simply pulled the fabric aside with his left hand. Ellen pressed against the tile, arching her bottom, raising it. She grabbed him, directing him.

"There?" he asked.

"Yes," she said. "Careful."

By March, it was still cold. It did not let up. In February, Ben and Ellen had taken Tom to the dentist when two of his teeth, molars, had simply fallen out. A few weeks later, he'd suffered from a bad rash across his arms, and Ben had waited for him at the dermatologist, who said he had eczema, and, moreover, needed to take a vitamin supplement. She recommended he see a general practitioner—he didn't look well. Several weeks after that, Tom's eye went pink and they took him to a different doctor, who said he had conjunctivitis.

They were surprised, then, when one morning Tom announced

that he was nearing completion of his project. Somehow, he had finished it early.

"I didn't know—I thought you said it was going badly," Ben said.

"It was. I mean, is. But there were a couple weeks there where I wasn't sleeping. I just plowed through it."

Tom sat in his chair. The collar of his T-shirt hung below his neck. His clavicles were visible, the deep well of his throat tight.

"I'm going to hand it in. I'm just going to do it. I think—I think I just have to get this thing done with. Once it's in, then I can relax. Kristin—well, she hasn't been around at all. I've been—I know that I need to pay her better attention. I know that," he said, looking up at Ben.

"Okay. Don't worry, pal. You're going to get this thing in. It's going to be terrific. You'll let me read it?"

"Oh, man, would you? Would you mind, Ben? I just—I wanted to ask, but I wasn't sure if you had the time. I know it's an imposition, but I mean, I'd be grateful. I really would."

That night, after work, after Ben and Ellen spent two hours with Tom at the pool, they read what Tom had given them. It was awful. The writing itself was so poor; it seemed to be simply a version of Tom's thoughts emptied out onto the page. Ben and Ellen were close—it was still cold. They were in bed, naked. They didn't laugh; they didn't make fun. Even Ellen, who herself was a bad writer, could see all the ways in which this would doom Tom.

The following day, she left it on his doorstep. There was a note: *Great! Send it in! We'll celebrate when you're done.*

He looked at it. There were a few edits—it was clear they'd read it. Which was very generous of them. He himself couldn't bear to look at it any longer. He changed it quickly and sent it in.

The remarks he received were damning. His boss said he didn't really have the time to go over it in detail. It simply wasn't working out. Perhaps they might just part ways. He didn't show the comments to Ben and Ellen. He was ashamed. It only confirmed what he already knew. Kristin wasn't home—she was working part-time with that guy Steve on the days she didn't have class. She said he was really, really sharp. He was going to get her a job, she was sure of it.

He set the papers down on the coffee table. He called his friend, the groom whose wedding he had gone to those months ago. He didn't answer. He wanted to call his father, but he would have to explain, which would be too much. His father had never wanted him to leave Chicago in the first place. Since moving, Tom had lost twenty-two pounds.

Finally, in the evening, he knocked on Ben and Ellen's door. Ellen answered.

"Hey," she said. She was wearing a pair of running shorts. Her legs were tanned somehow. She had on a tank top. Her arms had tightened. "What's up?"

"I just wanted to come by," he said. "I feel like I haven't seen you guys in forever."

In fact, it had been a few weeks since they'd all gotten together. Over the winter, when Kristin was working, they had been keeping up their routine, but Tom seemed less a part of it—Ben and Ellen had it down. Ellen had said that she needed to work late for a time, and Ben was juggling multiple projects himself, working toward building his own client list, and so they put a temporary hold on their evening swims.

"Oh," she said. "Okay. Come in, Tom."

"Is Ben around?"

"Yeah. Let me get him."

She went into the office. Tom could hear her say something to him. He couldn't tell what. They walked out as if they were addressing some bad news.

"Hey," Ben said. He wasn't wearing a shirt. There had been a break in the weather. It was warm. Ben looked very much like a boy Tom had once played baseball with, a second baseman.

"I figured I'd pop in on you guys. You know. Say hi."

"Sure," Ben said.

"Maybe you guys—I mean, if you're not busy, do you want to go down to the park? I have this Frisbee—it glows in the dark. We can toss it around. I don't know. I just felt like getting out. It's probably a dumb idea, but I thought I'd ask."

They looked at each other. They seemed inconvenienced. But they said okay.

At the park, where six months ago Ben struggled to do even one length of a farmer's lunge, they tossed the Frisbee around. Tom's vision had worsened—the cars' lights were disorienting. After five minutes, he was dizzy and said he was going to take a break. They should play, he said.

He sat on a bench and watched them. They were fast. They were fifty feet apart, Ben and Ellen, and the Frisbee would float beyond them, but they could catch it. They were pressing each other back, farther and farther.

He knew that Kristin was sleeping with that guy Steve. Four times she'd not come home, saying she had to pull all-nighters at the law library. At first, he believed her.

Ellen let out a shout, and Ben raced across the dead grass, vapor coming out of their mouths like wolves racing to feed. Their speed was alarming. He didn't have what Ben and Ellen did, and that kind of intelligence was required. Especially here, in this city. Right now, if he were out west, it would be warm. He would again be among friends. It would be another move, but he shouldn't think of it as a failure. Possibly, he'd take off for someplace else entirely. Soon, it'd be spring, full on.

"You're not going to catch me," Ben yelled at Ellen, who stood, hands on her knees, out of breath but smiling. "No way."

Tom moved out. He did not tell Ben and Ellen. Kristin had already left, had moved in with Steve. Which was no surprise. That was his talent. Ben knew it when they first met, where at a bar he left with two girls.

It was May. Ellen had received a promotion at work. Ben had

started his own consulting business, and several movie studios had contracted with him to do work. He had taken a number of clients away from his old boss.

Saturday morning, they woke up early to go to the farmers' market. Tom's apartment was open. There were two women cleaning it out, in preparation for it being shown to prospective renters. There was a small pile of trash—papers, receipts, some plastic shelving—outside the apartment.

"Don't worry. We clean it," one of the women said when she saw Ben and Ellen staring at it.

"That's okay," Ben said.

Amid the pile was the sheet of a client proposal Ben had shared with Tom. *If the IOC will be the church, the athletes themselves will be the priest class, and in order to enjoy the pleasure of watching them, spectators will pay a significant tithe.*

They left, walked out of the building, heading south toward the circle. They passed their neighbor, the old woman, near the entryway. She was talking to her dog as if it were a man. She looked up at Ben and Ellen. She did not recognize them. They strode down the street quickly. They were, she thought, a very handsome young couple. She was pleased to have them as neighbors.

THE NORTHERNMOST POINT

T HIS MAN who was visiting our friends—Tom. He knew them from college. He was talking about how it was difficult to find someone. How dating was very difficult. None of us could believe it. I know I certainly didn't understand it.

Tom said how it was just that the city where he had recently moved was pretty small. He felt he had done everything he could, and had dated every reasonable woman, and some not so reasonable, and was out of options.

It was summer and we were in a boat on the water. Tom sat at the bow, near my husband and my friend Sarah and her husband, Brian. Brian was his dear friend. Tom was the kind of man who had many dear friends, the kind of man one wants to call a dear friend. To hear him tell about his difficulties, and to look at him against the water—it was just hard to imagine.

He had dark, thick hair, a clean, handsome face. His arms—they were the arms of a blacksmith, though he said he was doing finance. Sarah had told me he had been an athlete in college.

"I don't know," Tom said, his voice rising. "I'll tell you, I've given it a shot. I feel as if I've given it *more* than a fair shot. But I think I may just be a bachelor from now on."

Brian said, "If anyone has given it a chance, you have. There was that one girl—I don't mean to sound cruel or anything—but she worked in a grade-school cafeteria. Right?"

"It was middle school," Tom said.

"Right. Middle school. A middle-school café queen. And she had that thing—what did you call it?"

"It was like a yip," Tom said.

"A what?" Sarah asked.

"Like a tic," Tom explained. "I almost got into a fight in a movie theater over it. She would let out this loud *Yip!* every ten seconds or so. This guy behind us wanted her to shut up, but I told him—well, I said some things to him. It wasn't right, what he said. But she said she didn't want to date me. She said I was too different from her."

"Wait," I said. "She didn't want to go out with *you*?"

"I guess not."

Tom reached down between his legs and pulled out beer from under the floor of the boat. He poured the beer into red cups, taking the last one for himself.

"Then there was the one from last year," Brian said, "Janie, who couldn't get over that you didn't hunt. I honestly don't know why you're out there, Tom. I mean, why was she so surprised that you wouldn't want to go hunting with her dad? What was his name, Buck Senior?"

Tom just shook his head.

"What happened with these women?" I asked.

"Nothing. That's what happened. You know, I actually went hunting with Buck Senior. We shot birds. In fact, I'm still in touch with him. I bundled his four-oh-one(k)s. I put him into a bunch of annuities. He was a foreman at a paper processor."

We were out in the deep bowl of the lake. It was about five o'clock—a Sunday. Tom looked out at the water, at the shore, at the tree line. I had heard that he had been with a lot of women, Sarah had told me, but was making a good effort at reformation. He was like a rehabilitated gambler. There were stories, Sarah said. Legendary.

Now he just seemed like a regular guy. He was in the white T-shirt. It had the name of a whiskey on it. He was in leather sandals. His legs were nearly hairless, muscular like a cyclist's. You could see him—a vision of him—on a bike rolling down hills in the mountains. All alone, though. He wore a class ring with a ruby in the center—it was from the university he went to with Brian and Sarah.

Brian asked if Tom wanted to drive the boat and Tom said okay. He took his beer over with him.

"No drunk boating," I said to him as he walked away from the bow.

He saluted me. "Aye, aye, captain."

"Maybe I should sort of conavigate, so that I can be sure we don't run aground of any icebergs," I said.

"That's right," my husband said. "Deidre was in the Girl Scouts. She did Outward Bound when she was in high school."

"What do you do now?" Tom asked as we settled into chairs next to each other.

"Oh, I'm an attorney."

"What kind?"

"I do health-care law," I said.

"What does that mean? Like pharma?"

I was a little surprised. In fact, my largest client, a client who was recruiting me to work in-house for them, *was* a large pharmaceutical manufacturer.

"You got it," I said. "I'm with the bad guys."

"I didn't say that," Tom said. He rested his beer in the small cup holder near the throttle. He stretched out his arm, and veins rode up and down it. "You said that. I think everyone deserves their day in court. That's what I think," he said.

"That's what *he* thinks," I said, pointing to my husband, who was a public defender.

Tom had one long leg up against the plastic console on which the wheel rested. He turned away to look back at how far we had come. The sky was darkening and a vapor was beginning to form on the water. Sarah's husband got up to turn on the boat lights.

"Are we okay, Brian?" Tom asked. "Gilligan here said this is nothing like the North Atlantic in December."

"Are you still okay, Deidre?" Sarah asked.

"Of course I am. Please. I just had a hand in successfully defending the Northeast's largest class-action suit. I think I can navigate a boat around a man-made lake."

Tom was impressed by this, I could tell. My husband often had mixed feelings about my saying these things, talking about work, which he didn't feel—he would never say this, but I inferred it—was not altogether virtuous. For a long time, this fact—the nature of our jobs—was important, and offered a place for debate. We saw this all as a positive, something that colored our relationship in an interesting way. We were a couple who could engage, even argue.

"That sounds like a big deal," Tom said. He poured a little of his beer into my cup.

"Well, I guess it was. It was a big deal."

"Congratulations."

"I should say—I mean, I don't want to sound like some kind of robot, but the case really was baseless. I just want to say that."

Tom looked at me. He didn't say anything.

"So, Tom, what do you think the problem is?" I asked.

"The problem with what?"

"With why you can't find someone?"

"Oh, *that*."

"I didn't want to sound—I didn't mean it like that."

"No, I was just confused. I was just confused for a second, Deidre. The reason I can't find someone? I don't know, to be honest. If I knew, I'd fix it, I guess. It's not that I'm looking for the perfect woman in the world. Well, I guess my story makes that clear," he said. "But I don't know. I'm willing to be flexible. I think that's important. But maybe it's like they say—timing. Have you got any hints?"

I didn't have any hints for Tom. There seemed nothing that he could do that would need to be improved upon. He got up for a second and said he was listening, and went to the bow of the boat to get more beer. He got one for me, too. My husband looked at us. He wasn't jealous. We had been married seven years. He once told me that under no circumstances would he ever *be* jealous of me, because that would imply that he had some kind of control over the matter. If I made a—this was his word—*digression,* then that would be on me. It wasn't something that he could predict, or hedge against, or be worried about. Our unity was strong, which was the reason we could have the dialogue we did—say the things we sometimes said. That was how strong we were.

"I don't have advice for you, Tom. Are you doing the online thing?"

"Tried it," he said, looking at me while he was turning us away from the shore, keeping us a safe distance from the docks that stood out from the land.

"Speed dating?"

"Yep."

"Hmm. I'll have to think."

"Don't bother," he said. "I've tried relationship sites. Dating sites. Marriage sites. Religion sites, even though I'm not affiliated. Sports sites. I even—I'm just saying this to illustrate something—tried a sex site. Just to see if I could meet anyone. You don't realize how small a city is until you try to date there."

"How did the sex one go?"

"The sex site?" Brian said. "Is that what you're talking about? The dating site Tommy went on? Oh, boy. *That* was the one. Was she ever the one?"

"What?" my husband said.

Brian—this was something we knew—was on his fifth drink since we'd arrived.

"Nothing. It was nothing," Tom said, smiling.

"*What?* It was *something.* Tell them. You tell them or I will," Brian said.

"It was nothing. I met a couple people, but it didn't work out. That's all."

"Oh, no," Brian said, and moved closer to the starboard side, where there was a seat. The vapor—they told us this happened—was thickening over the water. Tom was still driving. He slowed the boat down considerably. Every once in a while, he would honk the boat's horn, so that if someone were out there, they could hear us.

"Tell them about the two Marys."

"I don't want to," Tom said. He was a little upset. You could tell this.

"Then I will. The two Marys story goes like this."

Brian explained that Tom's on the sex dating site, but he's trying to meet someone for real. It's hard, but Tom is convinced that he can find someone whom he can have a life with. Even if the foundation is sex, which he doesn't necessarily have a problem with or want to be judgmental about, he can make something work. He has faith. You wouldn't know it, Brian explained, but Tom is sort of religious. Well, more spiritual. He even makes a point to put this on his pro-file. *Very spiritual.*

But you have to rule certain people out.

"The women," Brian said, "who e-mail and the first thing they ask is if your cock is bigger than eight inches—you rule those women out."

"Why do you rule them out?" I asked.

"Because they're men," Tom said.

The women who have pictures of themselves totally nude—them you can rule out as well, apparently, Brian explained. The women who want to talk dirty online—rule them out. Same reason—they're really men.

"But our man Tommy here, he finds this one girl, Mary. They e-mail back and forth. The picture of her—let me just say—can I say this, Tommy?"

"I don't think I can stop you," Tom said.

"Let's say that she's pretty. Maybe not as pretty as the women Tom, uh, well, *knew* before moving out there, but not bad. He sent me the photo. Not bad."

They e-mail for about a week before they set something up. It seems good. She's friendly, demure, funny even. Finally, she asks Tom if he wants to go out on a proper date.

So they set up a date. They meet at Tom's favorite bar. It's semi-upscale and is maybe one of the only classy places in the city he's living in. Right up against the mountains. Very pleasant atmosphere. They have their own specialty martini—the VO$_2$ max. It's actually named after Tommy, Brian explained.

"What does it mean?"

"It's how much oxygen gets through the body while exercising," Tom said. "The higher your VO$_2$ max, the better."

"What is yours?" Sarah asked.

"Uh, well, it's about fifty. Close."

"Is that good?" I asked.

"Fuck yeah," Brian said.

So he meets this girl Mary there. And she's not bad. She's pretty. She's not wearing something that would embarrass you if you brought her home to your mom. Chestnut hair, nice tits, good can is how Brian put it. Pretty.

They sit out on this deck overlooking the mountains and the forest. It's nice out. They even have heat lamps. It's one of these old hotels that rich people used to go to, and sometimes presidents, too.

They shake hands and Tom orders them drinks. Tom is trying to be especially gentlemanly. Mary is really nice. She's a pretty good girl. Not as gorgeous as back in the old glory days, Brian repeated, but still. They talk. They have one drink and then another. She tells about her life. She's a college adviser. Has her Ph.D. from Berkeley. She's real sharp. They talk for a time about the market. She wants to know about Tom. Does he have any free advice? Like what to do with her portfolio. It seems important that she ask about him. That she be interested in what he does, his life.

"What did you tell her?" I asked.

"I told her the same thing I would tell anyone. The same thing I'd tell you. Diversify. Have nine months available in cash. Don't buy real estate unless you're going to live there. The usual stuff."

"Conservative," I said.

"Yeah, well, here's how conservative our man Tom is," Brian said.

They get round after round of drinks. The sun is going down over the mountains and there's this smell of aspen and alder and smoke. Mary—she's getting pretty drunk. They get appetizers. The evening is going on. Finally, they talk about why they're on a sex site. She admits that it's just too hard to meet people, and she was fed up with dating and just wanted to give something else a shot. The same reason as Tommy.

"So far so good, right?" Brian said.

So they talk a bit about sex. Nothing explicit—that's not what Mary is about. She asks Tom what his best sex story is, and he says something dismissive, about how he once did it in an airplane, even though Brian told us that Tom really has stories that would outdo any dedicated sex site–goer. But he's a good guy now and is not going to say.

Tom asks Mary, but she gets a little bashful and says something about how it's not really a story, but more a funny thing, which is what her Vietnamese aesthetician—one she had when she lived in San Francisco—would say after a bikini waxing, holding a mirror up for Mary to see: "You fancy. You like Hollywood star."

They have some laughs at this. I can see Tom laughing, his lips pulled back, exposing the whitest teeth, teeth that are thick and very bright in the low light, sparkling red from the heat lamps.

They talk more about their lives. Mary about her work, about her parents in Palm Springs, about how she, too, likes to hike and bike. They share other things. Tom is originally from the Midwest and Mary is from California, which makes them both transplants. They both feel a little alien out there. They were about the same age. They are making a list; they are unifying. They talk about their parents, who are getting older, the matter of limited time. Some about politics—them being liberals in a conservative place, an attitude among the students she works with at the university that she doesn't like that much. Neither has siblings. They talk about themselves as kids. Tom was an overscheduled little athlete. He doesn't add about his achievements in college—he leaves those behind him. Mary says she used to be a thespian.

"You Hollywood star," Tom says. "You famous."

Mary laughs. They both do. They've had a good date; they joke about maybe writing in to the sex site about how a match has been made.

"Finally, she says—what did she say, Tommy?" Brian asked.

"She said that if I lived close, we could finish our conversation at my place."

"Good," I said.

"Right, good." Brian said. "You'd *think* it's good."

So, Mary says she's going to call a friend—she has this friend she wants to call, just to tell her that she is going back to this guy Tom's place, and that he is a good guy and all, and not a creep. And she is going to go to the bathroom. To freshen up and all that. Tom says he'll get the check.

So Mary goes to the bathroom. But—and Tom can see this— there's a long line. It's now high time for the bar. Everyone has a VO_2 max. It's buzzing. He wants to get the check. But there's a long wait now where they are seated, out on the deck.

So Tom goes up to the bar. He's waiting for the bartender to run their tab, and there's this woman seated next to him.

"The reason he even noticed her," Brian explained, "was that he had to practically fold himself in half to get to the bar. That's how big she was."

Tom shook his head when Brian said this. This was his friend from college. He couldn't make him accountable. Maybe Brian pulled Tom out of a mess before. Maybe he owed him in some way.

"Guess what her name is?"

"Mary," I said.

"Right."

"So this Mary—let's call her Big Mary," Brian said, "Mary Two. Mary double-wide—"

"I don't know if I like this kind of talk," Sarah said. "Maybe you could tone it down, Brian."

"What? Tom doesn't mind," Brian said, standing up. "Do you, Tom? She was a big girl, right?"

"Yeah, but that's not the point," Tom said. He looked out beyond the boat, and honked the horn loudly. But no one was there.

"How big was she?" my husband asked.

"Oh, boy," Brian said, spreading his arms out. "Like *big*. Like you and me combined."

"That *is* big," my husband said.

"Okay," Tom said. "Maybe we don't—" He honked the horn again.

"Well, I'm going to tell the story. I think there's a modern lesson here," Brian said, laughing.

Which is that after a few minutes of waiting for the bartender to come by, Mary II starts to chat up Tom. She's all alone. Happy hour. She's drinking a VO_2 max, too! And Tom talks to her. He's finally got the bartender ringing his tab, but the register runs out of paper. Mary number one is still waiting for the bathroom.

By now, Mary II is coming on strong. It's impressive, really. She's got nothing to lose. She outweighs Tom easily; she's *not* the kind of girl, Brian explained, you'd bring home to your mom, or introduce to your friends—not without some funny looks—but she's forward and she's nice enough. Nice enough for Tom.

After small talk, she says, "I saw you were with someone, but maybe you'd want to—well, maybe you'd want to connect with me some other time," is what she says, Brian explained.

"Do you believe this?" Brian asked us. "What does she care? She doesn't."

Tom stands there for a second, disbelieving. All these people in this bar are around him; the place is loud, the lights strange, the altitude strange. He's drunk.

What he realizes is this: Things with Mary number one, in all probability, won't work out. He might take her home. He might sleep with her. They might date for a bit. But even if *all* that happens, then the odds—and it's just *odds*—of them working out are not good. And then the disappointment. The grave disappointment.

Tom there at the bar, a man who any woman would look at and think he was handsome, and would be proud to be with, and who has the prudence to withhold judgment of a girl like Mary II—he takes her number.

"Maybe he'll call her, maybe not. But it's just an odds game. It's just the *odds,*" Brian said again.

Tom, still driving the boat, was not smiling. He looked sad. Sad and, moreover, confused. He wondered—he *must* have wondered—how things might have changed. Sarah told me that by the time he was twenty-two, he had already been with more women than Brian and she would ever be with people in their lives, and just to be clear, she said, these weren't the kinds of girls that you might think. These were women just like us, Sarah told me. Smart, pretty girls. You wouldn't think so at first, but it was true.

But this is more than a decade on, and here is this one girl, whom he had to meet on a sex site, waiting for him, and he's dated who knows how many, and is ready to settle down. He wants a life. And he knows that you couldn't expect someone perfect. He doesn't care about that.

He takes Mary number one home.

"What happened?" I asked.

"What happened?" Brian said. We were at the edge of the lake, the northernmost point of the lake, far from the house. "Tom. Do you want to tell them?"

"No," Tom said. He honked the horn again as he turned the boat around.

They *do* sleep together that night. And they date for a bit. Restaurants, hiking, but they always spend time at Tom's place. Which is fine, but a little strange. After a month or so, Tom, who doesn't want to be intrusive in any way, says that maybe they could spend time at Mary's place. Or he could see it. He doesn't want to press her—he is very careful on this point—but it seems, well, just normal that he should see her place.

So they go finally. And it's a lovely home. It's a nice house overlooking the mountains. It's a place that Tom can see himself in. Having a drink. He and Mary relaxing, reading the paper on Sunday. At night, them getting high. That sort of thing. He'd chop wood for this great adobe fireplace she has. The kind of place where Indian rugs hang on the wall.

Only, all around the house, Brian explained, there are pictures of this man. The kind that one would have done professionally. Portraits of this fellow's face in black-and-white. Tom asks who this guy is.

It turns out that Mary had been married before. It's her husband, she explains offhandedly. "Oh him? That was my husband, Darren." He had been an Olympic skier or something. No kidding. This husband—he was a wonderful man, she explains—had been driving with their young son.

"Wait," I said, "she had a husband *and* a son?"

"Right," Brian said.

They were driving and there was an accident.

"Imagine," Brian said, "losing your husband *and* your kid?" It's the sort of thing, Brian acknowledged, that one doesn't shake off—not ever.

"Well," I said, "I could see why she might not tell that. I could understand that."

"Okay, fine, but guess who the husband looked like?" Brian said.

I looked at Tom. He was playing with his ring, turning it around on his finger. He smacked the horn once, twice.

"It was like Tom had a twin," Brian said. "Isn't that what you said, Tom?"

"Yeah."

"He called me," Brian said. "'I have a twin brother' is what he said. The big nose, dark hair, everything. I told him right then to run for the fucking hills. This is the kind of shit you don't want to mess with. But does he listen?"

"No," my husband said.

"Right!" Brian said. "Because our man Tom, he's not the one who breaks it off. Tom is able to look past all this. The fact that this fucked-up lady is dating a guy who looks like her dead husband—Tom can work around it. They talked about him, the dead husband—he and Mary. He listened to her. She didn't say *anything* about the obvious fact that Tom looked like him.

"Instead, what happens is that Mary number one calls him a few weeks later—this is after a dozen good dates, or so Tom thinks—and just says, out of *nowhere,* she's met someone else. Not that she isn't ready for a relationship. Or that she isn't equipped. All of that we would understand. She's very sorry. He's such a great guy. She wishes him the best of luck."

"What did you do?" my husband asked.

"What did he *do?*" Brian said. "He called the Queen Mary II. That's what he did. And what do you think happened there?"

"No," I said.

"Yep," Brian said. "This cow, this fat fucking *cow*—I'm sorry, but I'm calling her that because I want to—this cow goes out with him twice, and he calls, and calls, and she just stops talking to him. She won't take his phone calls. Tom. Of all people! She won't take *his* phone calls."

"Okay," Tom said. "Maybe that's enough. I think you've offended enough people here."

Brian said, "You're the one who should be offended, friend. You're the one. Anyone would be lucky—no, *lucky* isn't the word. *Blessed* is the word. Anyone would be *blessed* to be with you. I've known you a long time, and I can say it."

"It's true, Tom," Sarah added.

"Well," Tom said, breathing in deeply. It was getting dark, and we could see the edge of the lake—trees hanging over the water, this quiet corner of the lake. The only light was from the side of the boat, and the dashboard light, and Tom's class ring. The only sound was from Tom honking the boat's horn.

"I think we're hungry," Sarah said. "We're going to make a store run to get a few things. Do you want to take us back, Tom?"

As we headed back, my husband and Brian and Sarah were talking. Tom said to me, "You know, I wouldn't have cared that much. That much about any of that stuff. The stuff he just told you. Mary's husband looking like me. It didn't matter that much. I'm going to be honest."

"No?"

"No. Not really. I'm not saying it didn't matter at all, but in the end, none of this was a deal breaker. You don't realize this until you're older. *I* didn't at least. These are not the things that matter. Where I live, you have to be open. You have to be willing."

At the house, Sarah made a list—what we needed for a barbecue. "More beer," Brian said. We were all going into Brian's big truck to go to the store. But not Tom. He was staying for the week, and he wanted to unpack. He was standing at the front door, and we were walking to the truck.

"You know what?" I said. "I think I'll stay here. I can—well, I can do some of the prep work."

"Huh?" my husband asked. "What prep work?"

"Yeah, there's really not that much you have to get ready right now," Sarah said.

"Well, someone should start the fire going. I can do that. So that the coals are all ready when you get back. Then we can just start."

Sarah looked at my husband. Tom was next to me.

"You guys won't be long, right?" I asked. "Like half an hour? It's close, the store. Isn't it?"

Brian got into the car and turned it on. Sarah smiled a little bit. My husband got in the backseat.

"We'll see you soon, Deirdre," he said.

I stood beside Tom. I looked down at his hands, and at the ring, which seemed very heavy, and whose stone, in the setting sun, now seemed yellow. They drove off and we went inside.

PRINCESS

H IS NEIGHBOR TELLS HIM this story. They've just finished playing tennis at the public courts. They're drinking water. They stand at the net, Tom's hip against the tape. He is in profile. The sun sinks, the light against his face.

This neighbor, Craig, is much older—sixty-two. He's a good guy. It happened many years ago, Craig explains.

He says there were four of them, dads who played tennis together. Right here, he says, these same courts. They all lived in the same neighborhood. They were a pretty good group. Played twice a week, from April up through September. Sometimes they'd get together for drinks.

They all had children the same age. Well, except for their buddy, Dick. He had twin boys. The other three dads had one daughter apiece. Two were nine and one was eight. They were in the same school together.

They decided one summer to do a camping trip: Craig and his daughter, Barbara, and the other two dads and their daughters. Dick decided to sit it out.

They pick a Saturday and the six of them head into the woods. It's a one-night camping trip. They bring two tents, one for the dads and one for the girls. Plenty of food: marshmallows and chocolate and graham crackers for s'mores, hot dogs, catsup. They bring beer, and one of the dads, Bruce, brings some grass. It's this really great American weekend they have planned.

It wasn't just Craig who felt it. They were all excited as hell. It was—well, it was like a little club. A fraternity. And it was nice, being with the girls alone, getting away from their wives. Really, he tells Tom, *they* were just kids.

"We were younger than you are now."

They were all coming up in the world. Craig had just opened his first tile store and things were going pretty well. Bruce was a lawyer with a shop that was doing a great business. The other dad, Pat, he had joined a practice of dermatologists. Starting to make some money.

They find a campsite in the woods. It's like another world up there. I mean, Craig explains, this is *way* up there. Anyhow, they're there by afternoon. They set up camp. He and Pat go collect firewood. Bruce sets up the tents, lays out the cooking gear, and watches the girls. He was really good with them, Craig explains. He was sweet. He and Pat, they sort of admired him for it. He was a little more seasoned than they were, had been married before. In fact, Bruce revealed to them one night after tennis that his little girl, Dana, was the child of this first wife.

The first wife was something else, Craig says. Niki. One *k*. Jesus. Bruce would tell stories. He and Niki when they were in their twenties. Them partying—they did just about everything, with anyone. And really, he would say, Niki was terrific. But in the end, she wasn't mother material. She knew it better than he did. There were certain things, Bruce explained—it just wasn't for her. Anyway, they divorced, and when Bruce met his second wife, Niki was okay with his taking Dana. They started a new life.

Pat didn't have such a great marriage. The rest of the group thought his wife was fine, though a little loud. She was from the East Coast. She was about twenty pounds overweight. She had these legs. Well. She was young, but they already had dimples. It bothered Pat. He was willing to admit it.

As Craig and Pat collect these branches, Pat says very quietly that he went recently to a bar that Bruce had said Niki spent a ton of time at to see if she was there. On a whim. Pat wanted to see her in the flesh. After everything Bruce had said, how could you not?

He didn't say anything to her, but he saw her, and she *was* something else. "I mean, really," Pat says. She had this dark hair. A body that you wouldn't believe. You thought about that, and the shit that Bruce had told them about her, and you didn't need much more. It was enough.

"Don't tell Bruce, okay?" Pat says.

"No problem," Craig says. "It's okay."

They continue to gather firewood.

"Really," Pat says, "I mean, I just wanted to *see*. That lucky motherfucker."

"I understand," Craig says.

It's near dusk, and they're all back at the campsite. The three girls are thrilled. I mean, Craig says, what's better in the world than being alone with your father? Nothing. They decide to play charades, father and daughter teams. Craig and his daughter go up first. The air seems full of vapor.

They're an octopus. They stand back-to-back in the light of this campfire Bruce has started, waving their arms, spinning around. It's really funny. Everyone is cracking up. The dads are drinking.

Then it's Pat and his daughter's turn. This tiny girl—Fern. Can you believe naming a kid that? Craig asks Tom. His wife insisted on it. Pat and Fern have a little meeting over by the tent, away from the fire, deciding what they're going to do. His daughter was the mousiest little girl. Timid. She didn't really fit in with the other two. You could tell that it really frustrated Pat.

He was the kind of guy who wanted to impress people. He was always stringing with natural gut. He even bought his own ball machine to practice when they couldn't get together. Had this Mercedes S-Class, though he said he was still paying off his med school loans. He had bragged about some big trip to Kapalua. He was a little guy. Had been a gymnast. Craig imagines nerdy Pat trying to hit on old Niki.

Anyhow, he's having this meeting with Fern, and his voice gets loud. Bruce and Craig look at each other. Pat finally drags Fern over and they stand next to each other and go about this bit—it's like they're chopping something. Their hands go up and down, up and down. The way the firelight is on Pat—he looks scary. And she— Fern—she seems sort of slow. Like maybe something is wrong with her.

They go on for about five minutes, and the whole time Craig and his daughter, and Bruce and Dana, they're guessing away. Are they making a cake? Are they supposed to be a scissors? I mean, they have no idea. It goes on for another five minutes, until Pat starts to grumble at his daughter—she's not doing it right. Bruce says that maybe they should just quit for the night so they can start in on dinner. It's getting pretty dark. Pat says okay, but you can tell he's disappointed with Fern.

Unwrapping everything, the daughters put their hot dogs on sticks that they've gathered and that Bruce has whittled a bit to make them good for cooking. Pat digs way down into this cooler. He says that he brought something special, a surprise, which is this bottle of twenty-year-old Macallan. He hands it over to Bruce so he can inspect it. They think his doing this is sort of strange, but hey, good scotch is good scotch. Pat had packed away some glasses, and they all pour a few fingers and sit back. The girls are talking among themselves.

And the men talk, too. About tennis, of course. Pat tells them about some new gear he's gonna get. Craig explains that Pat's looking at Bruce the whole time. I mean, Pat thought the guy was something else. He *was*, in a way. Bruce—funny, affable—and of course, he had that first wife. Princess, Pat calls her.

"Well, I don't know if she was much of a princess," Bruce says quietly, so as not to draw attention to the conversation. Maybe, Craig thinks, they hadn't told Dana yet. You never know with those things, and every family does it differently.

And then, right there with the girls roasting their hot dogs and chirping, Bruce starts to tell about how one year she arranged this special surprise birthday present for him. Her dad had this big boat. She brings him onto the boat, and what does he find? Four of her girlfriends, all there to wish big Bruce a happy birthday. Best birthday he ever had, he says.

Craig says that he was impressed, but, truth be told, he didn't necessarily believe it. Pat, however—he's just *staring* at Bruce. Holding his glass of scotch there, his hand shaking a little—he's paralyzed. Transfixed. To him, this is just beyond the pale. You could see him, right there by the fire, going through the whole evening of Bruce's birthday in his head.

"So?" says Pat.

"Well, yeah. I mean," Bruce says, looking at the girls, "maybe we can talk about it later?"

Bruce stands up and asks who's ready for s'mores. The girls have catsup on their lips; their hands are filthy. It was sweet, Craig says. Cute. You knew if the mothers were there, they'd be wiping the girls' hands and mouths every other minute, but the dads didn't care. They open up the packages of Hershey's and the marshmallows and graham crackers. They get everything ready. Bruce is really serious about making sure they're all set. The guy has the patience of a saint.

"Reminds me of you," Craig tells Tom.

As the girls start to roast their marshmallows, Bruce brings out this big bag of grass and his pipe, and he packs it and they take turns with it. Because, what the hell? The girls don't know. They're nine. They don't have a fucking clue. And they're passing it around. The night is so clear. Much was clean. They thought their lives were going in the right direction. There was a trajectory.

Only, at one point, Dana, Bruce's kid, lets out this scream. She's been burned. She drops her stick into the fire, leaps back, the graham cracker that had been in her lap flying—the marshmallow catches and burns blue and then is just this black lump.

She says that Fern pushed her.

"She burned me!"

Bruce puts the pipe down, gets up, but he's a laid-back guy, and he knows it's just his daughter being dramatic. So she cries for a minute, but he tells her that it's okay. He looks at Craig and Pat, a little embarrassed.

"Her mother's daughter," he says to them. "The drama queen."

Pat goes to little Fern and grabs her arm and asks her why she pushed Dana near the fire. She could have been hurt badly. Only, Fern doesn't know what he's talking about. Really, she didn't do anything, Craig says. Maybe it was an accident. But Pat—something is starting to unravel about the guy, and he shakes her really hard.

"You have to be more careful! Daddy's very disappointed," he yells, walking back to his folding chair.

The weird thing was that you could tell looking at Fern, this wasn't the first time she'd been through this with her dad. She sat back from the fire, curled up a little. It made you think, Craig says. What the hell was going on with them at home?

Craig says that maybe it's time for the girls to go to bed. But they don't want to go to bed. Well, Dana doesn't. She wants a ghost story. No ghost stories. Bed. But Dana wants one and Barbara says that she does, too, though she's just going along with Dana. Ghost stories. *Now,* they say.

Pat says that he has one. If he tells it, they'll go to bed? Yes, they say.

Craig doesn't think this is the best idea, and he tries to appeal to Bruce, but Bruce is pretty far gone at this point, and so just sort of shrugs his shoulders.

So Pat starts this story, very quietly, all spooky, about this family: mom, dad, sister—she's nine, he says—and a little brother. They live in a big mansion. Pat's really getting into it. But Craig is sort of worried that he's going to scare the crap out of the girls.

The story is about how on Halloween, the little girl hears something in the middle of the night. She goes downstairs. It's like a voice, calling her. She goes into the great room, where there's this very old fireplace, and she finds that a fire is going, roaring.

"Just like this one," Pat says, pointing to the fire.

The girl goes to sit in this old chair by the fire and a voice comes out of the fire. It says the name of the girl's brother. Over and over, it's saying his name.

"What was his name?" Dana asks.

"Daniel," Pat says.

"Oh, man," Dana says, excitedly. "Oh, boy."

"She goes back upstairs, the little girl, and the next morning, they find the brother dead. Dead, right there in his bed."

"How?" Dana asks.

Pat makes this noise, like a piece of paper tearing, and gestures, drawing his thumb across his throat.

Now, Craig, he sees where this is going, and he knows his kid pretty well. This is going to keep her up for nights. He gestures to Pat that maybe he shouldn't tell this particular story, but Pat smiles. It's no problem, he says.

"Right, gang?"

"Right!" Dana says.

So Pat goes on. He says that a year goes by. Halloween again. They all go to bed. Again, the little girl hears a voice. It's telling her to come downstairs. She does. Again, fire roaring in the great room. This time, the voice says the name of the mother.

"What's the mother's name?" Dana asks. She's loving this.

"Nicole," Pat says, smiling. Bruce doesn't quite get it, though.

"Sure enough," Pat says, "next day, mother's dead! Same way."

"Ok*ay,*" says Craig, clapping his hands together. "All righty."

"Hold on," Dana says. "I want to hear the rest of it."

The girls are practically wetting themselves.

"I'm telling you. I could see us up with Barbara for the next five years. I could see her in bed with us, I could see us at the child psychologist, and, friend, I could see the bills."

And almost worst of all, he starts to worry that the little tennis group, they're not going to be able to go on. Something was happening to threaten it.

"You don't have kids yet," he says, "but it was just this *thing*. It's different when you're married and you have kids, and manage to get a group of guys together. It's like—it's just not the same. You'll see, though," he says, looking down, tapping his racket on the net.

"I understand," Tom says.

Anyhow, Pat goes on with the story. The third Halloween, it's just the girl and her father. She hears the voice. This time, she hears her dad's name. Downstairs, fire roaring.

"No!" Dana says.

"Yes!" Pat says.

Sure enough, Pat says, the next day, father is found dead. In bed. Throat.

"And do you know what the police found when they arrived?" Pat asks.

"What?" Dana asks.

"They find the little girl, in her bed, all alone. A big butcher's knife in her hand!"

The girls scream. Pat's smiling. He's looking at Dana. She's smiling, too. Fern isn't, and Barbara isn't really, either.

"Great," Craig says. "Now, a promise is a promise. Time for bed."

They roll out all the sleeping bags and the girls go in and get all cozy and the dads stick their heads in the tent, and say good night. Fern asks if maybe they can leave a light on. Pat says that she's being silly. There are no lights in the woods. But Bruce says that it's no problem, and he rigs this little mini-flashlight from the top of tent.

"That's better," Fern says.

For a while, the dads sit around drinking some more of Pat's scotch and smoking a little more grass. The girls seem to be asleep.

Pat asks Bruce if he'll tell them the story of his birthday. With Niki and her four friends and the boat.

"What do you want to know?" Bruce says.

"Everything," Pat says.

So Bruce tells. He gives all the details.

"I guess," Craig says, "it wasn't a joke. This was stuff that you can't make up, you know?"

What Bruce says, though, is that even during it all, he never lost sight of Niki. It was like all these women were somehow less than she was. Inferior to her, he says.

"She was the one, huh?" Pat says. He's got this fiendish look.

"Yeah. I guess she was. Anyhow," Bruce says, taking this deep, reflective breath. "That's the way these things go."

By this point, the pipe is cashed and they're all beat. They decide to pack it in. Three dads, into this monster tent. It's Craig, then Pat, then Bruce. The night is quiet. Craig says he still remembers it perfectly. Remembers looking up at the sky before getting into the tent.

"You could see every star," he says. "Every single one. It was overwhelming."

Overall, he thinks, the trip *was* good. Maybe not perfect, but what ever is? He was glad that he knew these fellows. He felt as if he was a part of something. It can become very important, he says. He's sure Tom understands.

At some point—this is later—Craig wakes up. He's got to piss badly. He looks at his watch. It's three in the morning. He's drunk and he's stoned, but he says that he hears something outside the tent. It's two voices. He looks over and he sees that Pat's gone. Pat's outside, talking softly to someone.

So he gets up, opens the tent flap, and sees that Pat is standing with Dana, off a ways, beyond the campsite. They have their backs to him. Just these two figures. Their backs are just barely lit from the fire, which has died down. They could be father and daughter but are not. It's this man and this little girl. Standing still as statues. She had dark hair, just like old Niki.

He doesn't want to leave the tent. *Really* doesn't want to. It's just them two, standing side to side, facing the woods, looking down at something. What it is, he doesn't want to guess. They're perfectly still, except for a bit of the campfire light, which makes them appear as if they're quivering. Mostly, they're in shadow.

Craig makes this noise, like he's clearing his throat. He stands up. Pat turns his head, but Dana doesn't.

"Hey," Craig says.

"Hey," Pat says. "Hi." Dana is still looking into the forest.

"She was scared," Pat says. "She was crying. I was up. So."

"Okay," Craig says. He goes over to them. Still, he's a little hesitant. What are they looking at?

There's little Dana. She's got this expression, Craig says, like— empty. Not as if she's just been—you know—hurt. Just empty. She looks—*wise*. She looks as if she has already seen the world.

Pat—he touches Dana on the shoulder, whispering some final thing to her, and goes back into the tent, as if he's been put out somehow. Craig's just standing there with her.

He knows right then that Pat *did* go up to Niki. Went up to her at the bar. He can just see her amused smile as she sent him away. *Go on, little boy. Go.*

"Are you okay?" he asks Dana.

She looks up at him but doesn't say anything.

"Honey, are you okay?"

"Yeah," she says softly. He tells her to go to sleep. She goes back into her tent. He stands there for a minute, then goes into the woods. He's looking up at the sky. He tries to piss, but he can't. All those stars.

It takes ten minutes of standing out there until he can finally go. He's worried, of course, about what happened with Pat, but in a way, he's more sad. He's so very sad.

"I mean," he asks, "what the hell was I *supposed* to do? It was such a shame. The whole thing."

These men. He imagined them playing tennis ten years later, twenty. The fellowship. The secrets. Them at their kids' weddings. Them congratulating one another on grandchildren. Them as old men. When there was nothing else, there would be this. He could have it with Tom, but it'd be different: Tom's so much younger.

He went back to sleep, and the following day they went back home.

And though he never *really* knew what happened on that trip, what did happen was that they never got together again to play tennis. Poor Dick. He wanted to know why, *why,* but Craig couldn't explain.

A few months later, he heard through another neighbor that Pat had taken a job in New York. Bruce stayed on at his firm for a few years, made partner. They would see each other around, and they would chat, but that was it. Eventually, he got sick, the way all great men do.

Craig and his wife went to the funeral. They were greeted by Bruce's second wife, and there was Dana. The wife was crying. Dana wasn't.

"What about Niki?" Tom asks.

"I didn't see her. Not then at least."

He was out with a bunch of business associates. He was selling his chain. They were celebrating and came to the very bar where Bruce said he'd gone with Niki. It was the saddest thing, but there she was.

She sat at the bar, back erect, hair black, still long, though this was fifteen years later. She had on this loose black dress, cut low, so that you could see her shoulders, her spine—this great wonder.

They went up to the bar to order drinks.

"How did she look?"

He shook his head. No more.

He didn't speak to her. In a way, he hated her.

Tom looks down, runs his hands along the net, and takes a deep breath. He then looks up, beyond the court, the fence, the park. He nods his head.

"What's the old saying?" Craig says, smiling. He has kind eyes. His hair is mostly gone. " 'Good fences make good neighbors.' "

"Yeah," Tom says softly.

"I didn't mean to suggest—" he says, his arm out to Tom.

"Oh, no. I didn't take it that way."

"Anyhow," he says. "I envy you, Tom, in a way."

"How so?"

"You have your whole life before you. It's exciting. You've made a good start here. That's something, you know."

"Yeah, I guess it is."

"Not 'I guess.' It is. It's not the worst thing in the world to still be figuring it out. And it's not the worst thing in the world to get some distance. Certainly, Barbara has reminded me of that. I'm sure your father—well. I don't know, Tom. This is just based on some of the things you've mentioned. But you're in a good place now, don't you think?"

"Yeah," Tom says, and thinks about this for a second. "Yeah, I think you're right. At least it *feels* right." He faces Craig.

"It is. Believe me. Tell you what. I told you Barbara is moving back here?" he says. "She'll be by the house this weekend. You should come over. She'd love to meet you. I've told her about you."

"I'd be happy to," Tom says.

"I think you two—well. At least you should meet. She's bounced around a bit herself. You two are kindred spirits, I think. Oh, but do me a favor," he says. "Don't say anything to her about this."

"Okay," Tom says.

"I just—I doubt she'd even remember. But just don't mention it, okay?"

"No problem," Tom says, because it isn't.

HE TELLS HIS FATHER

H E TELLS HIS FATHER this girl is terrific. He can't wait for them to meet.

"She's a lawyer. She clerked for a Supreme Court justice. She told me that in his letter of recommendation he wrote that he thought of her as a daughter."

"Good, Tom," Stuart says. "That's—I'm impressed."

It's important that this newest girl be different. In the home from which his father speaks to him, one doesn't have to look far to find evidence of other women who seemed fantastic, but who ultimately failed Tom. Failed to measure up to his own greatness, his generosity.

On the dresser in his boyhood bedroom are pictures of his many dear friends, several pictures of girls he dated: a girl named Maggie with her arm around Tom on the Inca Trail, a snapshot of him and a date swing-dancing at a wedding. Another photograph from a time Tom lived in Boulder. This woman watches as he begins his descent down the slope, her mouth open.

When they have guests over to the house and Stuart gives them a tour, he takes them into Tom's room, where the pictures are prominently displayed. *And here's Tommy. Who's that with him? Oh, well—*

"When I come into town, I can meet her. I mean, that is, if you guys are still—you know. I'll take you guys out," Stuart says. "Of course, I'll want us to have some alone time, too. I mean, I hope that you can carve out some time just for us."

"Of course. I mean, look, it's still early. I know that. But—I have a feeling. It's just a sense. I was walking home from her place just a few minutes ago, and I thought, You know, this might be for real."

They chat a bit more. Stuart remarks on how long it has been since he saw Tom, though he has the sense Tom doesn't think it was long enough. Tom talks about how he is enjoying a new job. He has made his white-collar work itinerant and has never put down roots. Stuart speaks of some consulting he is doing to keep himself busy since retirement. He doesn't add that it would be good if Tom called more often.

It's late. Tom doesn't speak to his mother.

They hang up. Tom sets the phone down on his coffee table. He thinks that his father is proud of him. He fixes himself a scotch and soda and turns on the television.

The woman can redeem him in a way. He has only the vaguest sense that his previous failures have cast him in a bad light with his family and his friends. In fact, it's much worse than he knows. To Tom, every woman he meets could be the one—it's almost a motto. Often, there is a point later when he expresses "not feeling it"— something that seems to bewilder and make him sad.

As for him, they feel it too greatly. Tom is like an amusement park before it opens. Only later, sometimes years, when the lights dim, do the rust, litter, and the aching of the cars become evident. Before, however, there is the great speed, a curvature one rarely sees.

It is this quality that the newest woman, Diana, finds remarkable about him.

Tom was playing pool at a bar where her firm held weekly happy hours. She had gone reluctantly—an associate she was mentoring wanted to get her a drink. She watched Tom playing with several men she assumed were close friends of his, though in fact he had just met them. He would tell a joke; they'd laugh. The pretty bartender stood beside and laughed, too, the tray wedged between her hip and arm. Tom leaned over—the thin fabric of his T-shirt against his back, wide as a manta ray—levering the cue back and forth. Diana couldn't tell if he was thirty or forty. He might have been younger.

She had planned to go back up to her office. Tom was the first man she'd ever asked if she could buy a drink for. She spoke with him for an hour and then walked out with him.

"Diana," the young associate said, "didn't you want to finish going over the—"

"Tomorrow," she said.

That night, she sat naked Indian-style on his bed. He watched her. Her back was slouched; her breasts hung down. She was not young, but her body still seemed that way. She brushed her hands over the mattress, which was damp.

"I'm sorry," she said, smiling, a little embarrassed. "It's happened before, but—"

"Don't worry about it," Tom said.

"It's just when you did that," she said, looking down.

"It's fine. Really. I guess I should feel complimented."

She put her hands to her jaw and then on her knee—she was letting out her strings.

His apartment: The furniture was nearly crumbling—it was old, mismatched. There was a frayed T-shirt hanging out of his dresser drawer. Several letters scattered on his desk, the envelope flaps open, their edges sharp, the lips gummy. Dust on pictures of Tom and a man who must have been his father on a golf course, of them sailing, of them in box seats in a new stadium—they looked like colleagues. The dust on the frame of a panoramic photograph of Tom and nearly twenty friends, in shorts, before Window Rock. A small shot glass that read *Pura Vida!* Books whose spines faced away from her. A framed degree that lay on its side, atop still another degree. In her office, it was the first thing one noticed.

The following week, Tuesday, she called him to see if he wanted to get together again. He had not given her his number, but she didn't

think this was intentional. She understood it was simply an over-
sight. She had looked it up.

"Oh, hey," he said, surprised. "I didn't know if—yeah. That
sounds good. I'm getting out of here in five minutes anyhow. Why
don't we meet at five-thirty at—"

"I've got to finish up some things here," she said. "I'm working
with this young associate—she is such a pain. I've got to review a
few things with her. Why don't we do this—" And she suggested
they meet at 7:00 P.M. instead, far later than he'd hoped. She suggested a wine bar instead of the sports bar he'd had in mind.

"If you get there early, just go ahead and get us a table, Tom."

"Um. Okay. Sure," he said.

She showed up twenty minutes late. It wasn't a problem. He had
all the time in the world, and as he waited at the bar, he struck up
a conversation with the bartender, a tall young man with a dark
beard. He'd set before Tom a flight, which Tom was tasting from.
His knuckles were a threat to the stems. The bartender leaned over,
smiling, as Tom brought each glass to his lips.

When Diana came in, she kissed him on the cheek, asked if he'd
gotten them a table, realized he had not, and went over to one to sit
down. Tom went to pay the bartender, but the bartender said no.

"Have fun," he said. "Stop by again."

That date was a kind of triage, one she had done many times,
though the order of things in this instance, she would have to admit,
was reversed.

She wanted to know about his job (something in budgeting,
though he was not terribly articulate on what exactly), where in the
country he was from (all over, but raised in Chicago), what his parents did (his father was a retired real estate developer, his mother a
teacher), where he had gone to school (University of Arizona, where
he had played baseball—something she would have to make a dis-
pensation for; later UCLA), where he had traveled in the world
(everywhere—he'd built homes in Central America, taught English and math—but always there was the adventure). She inserted

a dozen other questions, though he was forthcoming on many subjects.

"I don't know, Diana. I'll say this: In my twenties, I really didn't care what I was doing. My job, what I was earning. Well, for the most part. But now"—he laughed—"I suppose it's somewhat different. I do want to finally—well, *settle down* is not the right term. How about *establish*? Can I say that? I want to establish something. Does that sound okay?"

She didn't know what to say to this. She felt the exact opposite. The entire purpose of her life had been to establish something, her reputation most importantly.

"You can say it, Tom. Of course you can say it. But—well. What do you mean when you say you 'didn't care'? I'm not sure I know what that means."

"Didn't care" meant that after he had finished his baseball career in college, he stayed to work in Arizona, mostly, he said, for a woman he believed he was in love with. After they split, he moved to Chicago, where he'd grown up and where his folks still lived, and worked there for a time. From Chicago, he left for L.A., then went to San Diego, then to Washington, and then to Colorado, of all places, where he put out his own shingle as a personal financial adviser, which didn't work out for reasons he didn't state. He tired of it after a couple of years. It was clear, in any event, these points weren't of interest to him. Mostly, he spoke of what he'd done, rather than what he'd accomplished.

She went on longer than he, sensing how inadequate she was in comparison to him. The list of her achievements was long, and Tom believed it would serve to prove that his own life up until now had not been a series of mistakes. He would acquire her accomplishments, which would show to everyone that he *was* serious, if only in a certain way. A woman like this wouldn't be with someone like him unless there was something substantive about him. No one could say that he wasn't a serious person.

————

He was thoughtful in the smallest, most obvious ways. He bought her a T-shirt so that she could play softball with him on Saturday mornings. He had it imprinted with *Counselor*. She declined. *You can go,* she said. *Of course, I'm not saying* you *can't play.*

After a couple weeks—she'd been assigned a big trial, the one she knew would make her career, and so needed most of her free time to work—he quit the league to spend time with her. He said he wanted to be with her while she worked through the weekends, if that was okay. They tried. She brought huge binders—it was a routine she'd done many times. Tom would bring a book and—she couldn't believe it—a journal.

Frequently, either on the street or at their table, there would be another woman: hair down, glasses, pashmina scarf. The girl, whom Diana would have dismissed in college, would examine Tom from a close distance, sometimes say something to him.

"Are you using this chair?" or "I see you ordered—is it good?"

"Um. Yeah," he'd say.

Tom had no idea what was happening.

"Pardon me," Diana said. "Excuse me." She leaned over the table, moving toward the woman. "Hi. Yeah." She walked away. "Thanks."

Tom continued to read.

A man will see a beautiful woman and say, *I'll leave with you right now. I'll leave everything I have.* He'll know nothing about her, but suddenly he's willing to devote himself to her. It was a woman's power, but Tom possessed it.

"Look, Tom. I just want you to know that if you want to be together, that's over." She pointed to the woman now leaving. "Okay? I understand that this can mean different things to different people. I appreciate that. But I just want to be clear with you so that there's no misunderstanding."

He smiled but didn't say anything.

"So, you understand that? Really. It's important that you do."

"Oh, of course," he said, laughing, shaking his head. "Yeah," but she couldn't tell if he agreed or not.

———

When there was time (Tom volunteered two nights a week at a church, teaching English to Spanish speakers), they'd go for walks together. For him, it was the slowing down and making permanent of their union. For Diana, it was like being seen with a celebrity. Anyone has a history, but Tom had a story.

He revealed the smallest details, which signaled to her there was a great deal more: a fly-fishing trip to Jackson Hole with his father, with whom, he indicated, he had a truculent relationship; a business retreat in Key West for a company he'd worked at for six months; a group of friends skiing in Banff; a group of friends hiking the South Rim. *A group of friends, a group of buddies, a buddy I know from, this dude I met, a guy I know from*—there were dozens, names that were indistinguishable; all of them seemed to her like vassals, the events like coronations.

And though Tom would never say it, and Diana would never ask, there would be all the women, and how when she now made love to him, she was surpassing them. She was coming to own the part of them they'd left with Tom, the part he'd acquired.

She had given him a key to her place. They didn't go to his apartment anymore. Returning from her office, she would find him outside her door, playing with two small children who, she believed, though was not sure, were her neighbors.

"Tommy, I want you to do this," a little boy said, pointing to the ceiling.

Tom took a soft pink ball and threw it against the wall; it banked off their door and down the hall. The little boy and girl raced for it. Tom sat against the door with his legs up, smiling.

"Oh, hey," he said to her. He stood up. "Do you know them?" Tom asked.

"No," she said.

"The little boy—Eduardo—he's eight. His sister, Anna, she's five."

The following morning, they knocked on the door at 8:00 A.M. to see if he could play with them. "No," she said. "He's still sleeping."

"Hey," he said.

"You're up?"

"C'mon, you guys," he said, taking them by the shoulders, drawing them into him. "Quietly. Just for a little bit."

They did this for many subsequent weeks.

He tells his father he can't wait to see him. It's been years since he's expressed anything close. Stuart, believing this reversal may be a result of this new girl, invites Tom to tell more about Diana: What did they do together?

Tom hesitates. "Well, she's working on this big case now at work. It's really—it takes up a lot of her time."

"Now, remind me. Where again is she from?"

Tom tells him, mentions where she grew up, makes a point to mention her academic trajectory.

"Boy. Wow. Well, that's exciting, Tom. How would you say things are going?"

"Very well. I think that I may not renew my lease when it comes up. She's got a place. It's a condo she owns."

"Huh."

"She said—this was interesting." Stuart could hear Tom taking a sip of a drink. He wished that he was beside him. It was his body, the effort of five hundred generations. "She said, 'You have your life: your job, your friends, the things that you do.' She said she'd never make me stop doing them. She's very independent. It's not like—well, it's different, for sure."

Stuart is alarmed by this—her thesis of Tom's life sounds purposeful and false. No one has ever managed to truly let him be, though they have all said they would try. Stuart just says, "It sounds like you guys are having fun."

"Fun? Dad, you're not . . ." he pauses.

He wants his father to acknowledge this, to say that he trusts

Tom's judgment, which would mean everything. Stuart tries to be modulated.

"Look Tom," Stuart says. "We're glad that you're happy. Of course. But I just want to make sure that you're not jumping into things too quickly. I don't want you to feel like you have to make something happen. I mean, after Kristin, I'm just a little concerned—"

"That was a long time ago. I knew that you'd bring it up."

"Look, I'm only saying. I hear "lawyer," and I think of her. I can't help but—I don't want you to get angry with me. But that girl—I mean, Jesus Christ—she couldn't stir your coffee. Everyone knew it."

These sentences kill Tom; they make him doubt himself. He thinks of his heart as something leathered, and with each setback in his life, scar tissue formed over a previous loss.

"Well, this is different. I don't know why you just won't believe it."

"Okay. Calm down. I believe it. I only want you to be happy, Tom."

"Okay. I know," Tom says.

It's true. Stuart's only wish is for his boy to be happy. For himself, he simply wants to witness Tom grow old, become more powerful, wiser, more fully the man he is beginning to demonstrate the qualities of.

"We'll have a good time when I get there. Can you make us some dinner reservations? Maybe you two could pick a place for Saturday night. It'd be nice."

When Stuart stepped out from under the lighted hotel awning, Diana did not realize that he was Tom's father. His face seemed disconnected from an age. He was tall and thin. He had dark hair, like Tom. He wore slacks and cordovan shoes, a sport coat and a white shirt. He looked as if he were waiting for a Town Car to pick him up. She could see that he was mostly a quiet man.

"Dad," Tom said.

Stuart turned slowly. The nose was the same.

"So," Stuart said, "this is the famous Diana."

"Diana Weiss," she said, sticking out her hand for Stuart to shake.

He was surprised. Instead, he simply hugged her. He smelled the same as Tom.

"Oh, dear," she said as she tried to adjust her footing. "Okay," she said softly. She put her hand on his hip. "Stuart," she said, "I hope that Italian is okay for you. I made a reservation at this brand-new place. You might have seen the chef on television."

"Diana," he said, releasing her, "whatever you recommend is good by us. Right, Tommy?"

"Oh, yeah," he said. "They eat pretty well at her firm, Dad. Diana, do you want to tell my dad about your big case? Dad, you've got to hear this. There's this one guy. He was some big shot trader out of Atlanta. He had this holding company—I mean, it's all over the news what this guy did. They finally bring him into custody, and they discover—"

"I want to hear about you two first. You can tell me about work later."

As they walked toward the restaurant, Diana let Tom speak. He tried to describe their calendar—what their life looked like in a week—but it came out sounding thin. A dinner on a Tuesday, a happy hour on a Friday, e-mails exchanged during the day, though mostly sent by him—she was so busy.

Sitting beside each other on the couch—elbow, wrist, and the smell of him—the time felt important to them both, but it wasn't something you could list, and to her, lists were everything.

Stuart stopped at the glass door of a French restaurant. Inside, it was crowded, people laughing, people's faces over large black pots.

"Tom," Stuart said. "Look. They have your drink."

Tom came up beside him. He chuckled.

"You know, it doesn't look bad here," Stuart said, stepping back, looking at the menu. "Have you guys ever been here?"

"Um, no," Tom said.

"How much time do we have? Do we have time for one drink?" Stuart asked, looking at the two. Tom looked at Diana.

"Um, sure. Sure, why not?" she said.

They went inside. It was bright and noisy. As they approached the bar, a couple got up to leave. Diana sat beside Stuart, and Tom stood. They ordered a round—no, Diana didn't want anything. Tom looked at her and she said okay, one glass of wine. Stuart chatted with the young woman bartender. Diana couldn't quite hear what he was saying. In addition to the drinks, to Diana's alarm, the bartender placed before them three shot glasses full of scotch.

"It's kind of a tradition," Tom whispered to her.

"Tom—I can't. You have it."

"To new beginnings and good memories," Stuart said. She could see him saying this, like a prayer a father will offer on Thanksgiving or Christmas, the little saying each family has, but not her own.

She took only a tiny sip. Soon, another seat opened up beside Stuart, and Tom sat down next to him. They ordered still another round of beer, Tom leaning back and saying to Diana, "Are you sure you don't want one?"

"No. Thank you."

Tom and Stuart talked, bent over their drinks, nodding their heads. She looked out toward the door. There was a line. There were many couples her age. Men in navy V-necked sweaters and collared shirts underneath, nice blue jeans. Expensive shoes. They took the coats off their wives and some pulled out the seats for them, though not all. Tables with people on double dates. Someone would tell a story, the rest would laugh. She didn't have many friends, but few people really enjoyed even one deep relationship.

"Tom, I think we should probably be going, don't you?"

Tom looked at his watch.

"Yeah, I guess you're—"

"Hey, let me propose something," Stuart said. "What if we just—"

And so they stayed. Tom and Stuart spoke briefly again with the bartender: "Absolutely, Stuart," she said. "I'll have it transferred."

"I hope this is okay," Tom said.

"Well, I should at least call to cancel the reservation," Diana said, but Tom didn't hear her and she didn't call.

They sat at a small table on the second floor. Soon, still another round of drinks appeared, and in addition, Stuart ordered a bottle of the house red.

Tom ordered a pot of mussels and it was brought out quickly. No, thanks, Diana said.

"Are you kidding? It's terrific," Tom said, already opening a shell.

"No, thanks," she said.

They ate that with bread, and then, when they were finished, sopped the liquid from the bottom of the pot with the bread. The entrées were brought; both Tom and his father ordered steak frites, Diana a small salad, though when it all arrived, Tom just shook his head. It wasn't going to be enough. Stuart agreed. So they ordered still another pot of mussels, and, Stuart decided, cassoulet, which someone would eat.

"What did you guys do today?" she asked.

Tom said they'd eaten lunch and then had hoped to catch the UCLA game at a bar, but—and Diana was surprised to hear this— Tom said it was too crowded, too many young people there, and so they had left for a bookstore.

"You were gone a long time."

They didn't say anything, just nodded.

"What in the world did you do there for four hours?"

"Oh," Stuart said, grinning. "We caught up."

Tom looked at him. She felt, though she didn't know why, that they had been speaking of her. That Stuart had been talking Tom out of being in love with her. *Why?* she thought to herself. Why would he do that? She was, in most ways, the woman whom one would *want* their son with. Perhaps—she could acknowledge this— there was the matter of her career, the depth and rigor of it—but with Tom, she'd seen it as a complement to his lack of one.

Diana said, "I heard that you sold your company not too long ago. It must be nice to have more time. It's hard for me to imagine."

It didn't come out sounding the way she'd wanted, as if she didn't have enough time for Tom, which was true.

Stuart only said, "Yeah, I would say the time is nice."

Diana said, "Tom said you were from Florida. I have an aunt and uncle down there. In Fort Lauderdale."

"Oh, yeah?" Stuart said. "I'm from a bit farther north. Jacksonville. Have you been there?"

"No," Diana said.

"You're not missing much," Stuart said.

They ate and drank. Mostly Tom and Stuart. Twice, Diana signaled to Tom to scoot his chair in—there were people trying to get by—they seemed to take up a great deal of space. The second time, she dragged Tom toward her. She said, "Here," and positioned him directly next to her, putting their hands together.

She imagined Tom and his father outside their home in the suburbs, a wood smoker going, a barbecue cooling, big cars in the garage; a vast home, a mother beside Stuart, and friends of the family, friends from the neighborhood, the great buddies of Tom, men all, oh, perhaps a couple women, women who had grown up with him but never fallen for him or just never so deeply that it was irreparable, understanding his limitations; golf in the afternoon and again the next day, them drinking and laughing, a gesture of Tom's ribboned arm raising a bottle of beer and setting it down, this repeated action like a salute.

She knew that she would never fit in. The long hours of sitting, the wood popping in the stone fireplace, the way they seemed to soak up each other's light—a quiet that felt like a criticism.

The meal was nearly finished, and Tom held his beer to his chest.

Stuart asked Tom, "How long do you think you're going to stay put?"

"Why?" Tom asked.

"I just wonder if you could be doing something more rewarding—I mean, professionally—than what they've got you doing now."

"It's not so bad," Tom said.

"I just think—well, it's not the money," Stuart said. "But it just doesn't sound as if you're as satisfied as you could be. That's all I'm saying."

"Oh, I'm not sure about that," Diana said. "Perhaps that's not entirely fair."

Tom looked at Diana.

"I mean, you seemed to have enjoyed it when you were on your own," Stuart said. "I know that it didn't quite work out the way you wanted, but that didn't have anything to do with the business. I would just say consider it again."

"I don't know," Diana said. "I want to see Tom do what he wants to do. If he wants to clock it in, that's fine with me. If eventually he wanted to quit working full-time, that would be okay, too. We all work too hard. I certainly do. I'd like to see Tom do what his heart is telling him to do."

Stuart just looked at her.

"I work enough for the both of us. I earn enough, too," she said, smiling. "Certainly, there would have to be an understanding about everything, but that's just—I mean, that's what being a partner is."

Tom looked down at his glass. It was finally empty.

It was late—when couples returned home to baby-sitters and twenty-four-year-olds were just going out.

"We should be getting home," Diana said. "Don't you think, Tom?"

"Yeah," he said. "Dad, I'll swing by at about eight A.M. to take you to the airport, okay?"

"Well," Stuart said. "Who said I'm ready to call it a night? It's eleven months since I've seen my kid, and I'm packing it in already?"

"I think Diana is tired, Dad," Tom said.

She didn't say anything right away. She looked at Tom. And Stuart didn't say anything. Nothing like *I understand. Of course. You two go on home.* He waited.

"It's okay, Tom," Diana said finally. "You two can stay out. That's all right."

"No," Tom said. "I can—"

"It's okay," she said. "You guys have fun. Just—will you please call me if you're going to be *really* late? Or text me?"

"I don't think we'll be *that* late," Tom said.

"I'll take care of him," Stuart said, putting his arm around Tom.

"Well, just be sure to let me know, okay?"

They walked for a ways. Tom did not look back to see Diana returning to her place.

"So?" Tom asked.

"So what?"

"So what did you think?"

"Oh, Tom," Stuart said, "you don't need my opinion. I mean, c'mon."

"Hmm. Well, at least, what was your impression?"

"She's nice. Quiet. She certainly seems to like you. She's very pretty. I don't know, Tom."

"And?"

"I don't know. I mean, one thing would be to just make sure that she understands that you're not going to quit what you've worked so hard at. I mean, I would make that clear."

"I don't think she was saying that."

"Well, I don't think she really appreciates that there needs to be"—he says *there needs to be* instead of *you need in your life*—"some organizing principle. That feels important."

"Yeah," Tom said.

They stopped talking.

"Do you remember that kid Matt Lisner?" Stuart asked.

"Yeah. We played baseball together."

"I see his father sometimes. He told me Matt used to live here."

"Oh, yeah? I think—I heard he was drying out."

"Really? Could be, but I don't think so. I saw him recently. He was with his father. He went to work with him. Nice kid."

Tom smiled.

"Boy. Well, maybe he's reformed himself."

"I said to him that I was coming to visit you here. He sent his regards. He said he was sorry you two hadn't been in touch. He wanted me to tell you."

"Good."

"In fact," Stuart said, looking up at the street signs, "he mentioned a place to me if we wanted a drink. I didn't want to suggest it in front of Diana. I didn't think she—well. But he said for us to check it out." Stuart told him the name.

"Sure. Yeah. It's a club. Well, sort of. I could see him at a place like that. But Dad, I think you need a reservation to get in. And—" He looked down at what they were wearing. In fact, he realized, they were dressed fine—they would be admitted.

"Do you want to check it out?" Stuart asked. "I'm not tired, for some reason."

Tom looked at his watch.

"Okay," he said.

It was a restaurant which turned itself over to a lounge late at night. They walked in. No one would have thought it looked odd.

"I'll find us a place to sit," Stuart said, and went over to a roped-off section toward the back. A bouncer stood beside it. Little cards on the black tables read *Reserved*. Tom went up to the bar to order them drinks. Stuart said something to the bouncer. He leaned over to listen to Stuart. Tom could not see, but the bouncer took a small list out of his pocket, crossed a name off, and then nodded.

He came up beside Tom. "We're all set. I've taken care of it," Stuart said. He gestured to the bartender and signaled that they would be moving.

It was dark and very noisy, but Stuart didn't seem bothered. He sat beside Tom on soft-cushioned benches. Their heads were close as if they were in counsel. *Yes,* they seemed to say to each other, *I know just how that is. It's so true. It was fun, wasn't it?*

After a time, a young woman who was holding a martini glass—she might have been twenty-five—sat down on the end of the sofa.

The bouncer had stepped away, but when he returned, he said to her, "Sorry, this whole area's reserved," and held out his hand to help her up.

"That's okay," Stuart said. "No, no. It's not a problem."

The young woman was surprised to hear that Stuart was Tom's father. She could see it—well, she could *kind* of see it. Her friends soon arrived and joined them all. Tom ordered a couple bottles for the table. He looked at Stuart when he did it. "Of course," Stuart said.

For an hour they talked. More women arrived. Tom told many stories about him and his dad. Few sons can tell a story about their father; Tom's were idolatrous. What little light there was found its way to Tom and Stuart: the large noses, the dark foreheads, the thinning, dark hair, the eyes, which displayed creases when they smiled, and they smiled a great deal.

Stuart put his hand on Tom's knee. He himself spoke to several of the girls alone. He did not condescend. He wanted to know about them. It was more than small talk, but never untoward. He spoke a lot about Tom. "The last good guy," he said, "though of course I'm biased," and they thought it could be true, and when Stuart got up to leave around 2:00 A.M., he bought a round of shots for the now dozen of them. "My parting gift!" he said. Tom got up and said, "What about tomorrow?" and Stuart said, "Stay. I'll take a cab to the airport," and he gave Tom a big hug. He kissed Tom on the cheek.

"Please," he said, gesturing to the space he left beside Tom, and they filled it in.

In the hours between when Stuart left and Tom returned home in the very early morning, well, Tom would feel a great regret over it. It was a mistake he had made before and it was foolish. He thought that he had grown out of all that. If anything, that part frustrated him the most. Of course, he'd tell Diana what had happened. He was too old not to.

She was very quiet. She looked up when he was finished, appeared to be taking an inventory of her condo: burnished metal fixtures, granite island, glass dining table, tiny sharp spotlights. She said he should go. He could stop by later and leave the key under the door. Never in her life did she say this, but to him, she said, "It's too bad."

He didn't bother to negotiate. He'd tell his father, crying, what had happened. Maybe Stuart would be pleased. Tom felt like a failure—he was no longer a kid. He wasn't sure he was going to get over it.

"That's silly," Stuart would say, and Tom would ask how he knew, and Stuart would say, "Because you always do."

He passed by the apartment where the children lived. What he could do, he figured, was write them a note when he dropped off her key. Their parents would bring them to his softball games on Saturdays in the fall and then again in the spring. In front of him, the elevator opened. He waited a second before he entered. They would make small presents for him, and after the game they'd sit in the bleachers and tell him about school. He looked back down the hall. There are phases, he reminded himself; stages one must pass through. After her, there would be the children. It would go on for some time, at least while he remained in the city. The elevator door began to close and he stepped inside.

Some months later, Diana was at her desk when someone knocked on the door to her office. It was late—8:00 p.m.—and she was getting ready to leave. She had been made partner, having won her case. She opened the door. A paralegal whose name she didn't know said that she'd accepted a package for her and handed Diana an arrangement of flowers—pansies and marigolds, in time for spring.

"Look at you," the woman said, smiling.

"Excuse me," Diana said, taking the package and closing the door.

She opened the small card. It was from Tom's father, Stuart. It simply read *Congratulations on your victory.*

She took the flowers and set them on her desk. They were pretty. She did not throw out the card. She kept it in the same place she kept the letter from her friend and mentor the justice.

COTILLION

S HE SAYS, "Your phone is ringing," and she hands it to him.
"Hey," he says, and then is quiet. "Jesus," and "God," and then
something that sounds sad but knowing, resigned, and then finally,
"Well, I mean, listen—okay. Yeah. Well, I don't—okay. I'll talk to
you."

"What *was* it?" she asks.

He explains that a very old friend of his—from when he was in
college—has died of a heart attack.

"A heart attack? How old was he?"

"My age."

"You're kidding me?" she says, hand up to her mouth.

"No."

"Who was it that called?"

"Will."

She knows him a little. A doctor. Met him first at a wedding she
and Ted went to in Santa Monica with all his old buddies. Saw him
another time when Will came to D.C. for a conference. He was a
nice guy, she recalls, though quiet. The three of them had gone out
for drinks at the Hay-Adams. Ted had thought Will would like it,
its decadence, though she couldn't for the life of her imagine why.
But he had been pleasant. Quiet.

"I'm sorry," she says. "Who was it that died?"

"Tom."

"I don't know him. I mean, you never mentioned him."

"Tom Mahoney? I didn't mention him? Sure I did."

"No, I don't think you did," she says.

She's confident she would remember. There is enough about him she doesn't know, and enough she would like to. A little more than a year in, now living together—how much about a person's life does one need to access? As little as possible, one of her friends had said, joking. How many karats—*that's* what you need to know, the friend had said.

"I'm so sorry. But I don't recall you mentioning him. Honest."

He's watching the World Series. He's in black Adidas warm-up pants and a shirt that advertises the Rose Bowl. Fall has grown cold quickly and the old vents expand with heat, give off the smell of warmth.

"Do you want to talk about it? We can."

"No," he says lightly, and smiles a little bit. "I hadn't heard from him in a while. Really, I don't know how long."

"Heard from who? Will or Tom?"

"Tom. I mean, the shit that this guy was into," he says, smiling. "My God. He was one of those guys, you know?"

"Oh," she says. She wants to know more but fears asking him because of the nature of it all.

She met Ted at a softball game where their two firms competed on the Ellipse. She thought she might have even heard of him before. A friend of hers was dating a guy who worked with him, wanted to set her up. His name—Ted Allison—that was what she remembered. Then she finally met him at that softball game, spring cracking open in the city; then the group of them, her friends and his, walking around the Tidal Basin, packed in the early spring with Asian tourists, the cherry blossoms pink and white. Photos of the young, good-looking couples and their friends, rosy-faced and cold but ready for the summer.

She told her best friend in New York at Cravath, her sister in Chicago, her parents in Ponte Vedra: I met a guy, a lawyer, Ted Allison. He's nice. Very sweet. Yes, he's cute. Really. Smart—very.

Older by a few years. Works at Sidley. I wouldn't say it's serious yet, though it could be. We're taking it slow. We're seeing how it goes. He's coming out of something, and of course there was Derek, so. Slow.

It started with that softball league and then a few happy hours. But then he took her to the Kennedy Center to hear the National Symphony Orchestra, to the Folger Shakespeare Theater for *Henry IV,* to Politics and Prose for a reading by an outspoken left-wing journalist. After a time, they didn't meet up with friends. They were dating without having even talked about it. Everyone knew and some were jealous of them. They went back to his place or hers.

He made love in a way that was better than she was used to. Not exceptional, though what did that really mean? It was good. Great at times. She told her sister this and her sister said, hang on, yelling for her children to get upstairs into bed right this minute. One month. Two. Is it serious *now?* her mother asked.

After eight months, they moved in together. His place, a condo in north Dupont. They saw little of each other at times, owing to work. Certain mornings, he would be gone altogether before she woke, his gym bag with him, and she would rise and go for an early run, leaving his place and then bursting through the ribbon of little children shuffling to day care across the street at Our Lady, Queen of the Americas.

"I have to go to his funeral," he says. "It's outside of Chicago. Where he grew up."

"Okay," she says. "When?"

"Saturday. I'd come back Sunday."

"Okay," she says.

He turns back toward the television. His legs are up on the dark wood table. Strong legs. He shakes his head a bit and says, as if remembering, "Oh, man. His father. Christ."

"What?"

"They were really—well . . . Nothing."

"Do you want to talk about it?"

He looks at her, though doesn't say anything.

"Okay," she says.

She goes to read. She goes to sleep.

She leaves work early the following day (the partner under whom she works is on vacation and had told her to) and goes to get a massage at her club with a friend. They talk, lying on their fronts. She says that one of Ted's friends died.

"Oh, my God," the friend says. "What did he die of?"

"A heart attack."

"*What?* Is that even possible?"

"Evidently. I think that the guy might have been into stuff. I don't know—I wasn't clear on it all."

"Oh God, Beth," her friend says. And then they are quiet. The sound of fingers on oiled, tan flesh.

"He's not that sad about it. I said that if he wanted to talk about it, we could, but he didn't really want to."

"Maybe they weren't that close."

"I don't know. Maybe. I just feel as if he *should* talk about it. You know?"

"Yeah."

This friend had been there from the beginning, knew that Beth and Ted made an outstanding couple. They even looked good together. One of those active, healthy, fun pairs. They hiked Old Rag together, Sunday brunches in Arlington at Whitlow's, beer and Bloody Mary's at noon. Beth was the girl who, if she earned an A- on a paper, would stay after class to argue for an A, which she would receive. She kept a perfect calendar. You never waited to receive a thank-you card from her, a holiday card, a phone call on your birthday. She gave much of herself and was now, with Ted, receiving her due, though it had been hard at times.

Prior to her birthday, Beth had slept with two men in one week, then on her birthday had wept among friends on the cab ride home. She had been engaged to Derek and now was starting all over. It wasn't the end of the world—she didn't want to sound dramatic. One friend in the cab worked for State on Darfur, one on human sex trafficking. She sounded frivolous and didn't want to, but maybe they could see. "I'm sorry," she said. "It's stupid."

"No, it's not," the friend had said. "I'm sorry. I shouldn't complain. Never," Beth said. "No, no," the friend insisted. "I totally hear where you're coming from." Which was true, she did.

The math was very easy. One year to get to know him, to be sure. One year for the engagement. One year as newlyweds, settling in, to work out the kinks. Then a first attempt, assuming it'd be a lucky one, turning into nine months.

"You know," the friend says, "Mike—he had testicular cancer when he was twenty-four. He won't talk about it, either. Absolutely will not."

"I didn't know that," Beth says, her throat tight, awkward.

"Well," the friend says, "he won't tell anyone. Though, of course, it doesn't come up. We do that walk once a year, but that's it. He has pictures—I've seen them at his parents' house—from when he was getting chemo, but honestly, you ask the guy about it, and he shuts the conversation down immediately. Won't entertain it."

"Why not?"

"I don't know," the friend says. "It was bad, for one. Had metastasized. And also, he just thinks that it was something that happened, and now it's over, no recurrence, and you have to move on from this stuff. I asked his mom about it once. All she said was, 'That was a hard time for him.'"

"Oh. That's awful. That's really awful."

"Listen, don't say anything to Ted about it."

"Of course not. No. Of course."

She turns her head away from her friend, her face against the leather table, looking at the wall.

That night, they meet friends for drinks. Some associates from her firm, other friends they know in common. Ted arrives a bit late. Told her he would be but didn't say why. They had all asked where he was—it was nearly eight—and she'd explained he was working but he hadn't made any indication to her what he was working *on.*

She sees him come in. He goes no farther than three or four steps before he catches the Celtics game on television and stops. His mouth is open a bit. In high school, he was a famous forward. His name was still up there, on a blue-and-white banner hanging in the gymnasium—he had shown her this when she went to visit his home. People had even come up to him in the stands and reminded him what a joy he had been to watch.

He goes over to the bartender, still half-looking at the game, and they begin to chat. The bartender tells Ted the score, how the game's unfolded so far. Ted orders a beer right there. Watches the game, looks around, finally sees her, indicates that he has already ordered, points with his finger to the bar, and waits for his beer.

She goes over to him.

"Hey," he says.

"You're late. We were all waiting for you. I didn't know what to tell people."

"This first-year needed some help with a brief."

"Who?"

"This guy—" And he's about to say his name, but doesn't. "He's new. How was your day off?" he asks. She asks if he knew that Mike had cancer and Ted says that he did know. He says he's surprised that she knew. The beer is placed before him and Ted reaches for his wallet, but Beth takes his hand and says to put it on her tab.

"Lucky guy," the bartender says.

"Come," she says, and he does.

"Look who I found," she announces.

While the group of friends talk about the election, talk about the new overrated, overpriced restaurant on Capitol Hill, talk about a mutual friend's bridal shower in Manhattan, Beth looks at him. It is as if nothing has happened. His shoulders are squared, his hair neat, his waist trim, a tiny, pleasant smile on his face. There is a layer around him. She has sensed it from the beginning. Impenetrable—a film of luster and mystique. In his company, at times, she is a little girl: frustrated, nearing a tantrum, wanting.

In an hour, they leave, walk home from the bar quietly. North on Connecticut, she holds on to him carefully, a little drunk.

"So, I'm leaving early," he says.

"Oh. I didn't know if you went ahead with it," she says curtly.

"I told you I was."

"But I didn't know if you were *actually* going to. I mean, it's not as if you were close. At least that is how it sounded. Or how it didn't sound."

He looks at her.

"Close enough," he says. "Everyone is going, and I have to, too."

"Did you find anything more out?"

"No, not really," he says.

"What do you mean 'not really'?"

"I mean I didn't," he says, smiling a bit at her.

"It's just strange."

"Yeah."

"I mean, what did Will say?"

"He didn't. You don't ask."

"What? Yes, of course you do."

She begins to walk ahead of him toward the condo. She opens the door before he does, walks up the short lobby ahead of him, even gets in the elevator and allows it to close, though he is quick and sticks his arm in, and the door bounces back.

"What the fuck?"

"I want you to tell me what is going on with you," she says, close to crying. "You won't say anything."

"Maybe I don't want to."

"Maybe you *should*," she says. "I mean, you knew this guy and you were what—friends? Good friends? Really," she says, out of breath.

"Yes. We were good friends. He was a good guy. He liked to have a good time. That's it."

"What do you mean, 'have a good time'? I don't know what that means."

"It doesn't mean anything. You had a good time around him. What difference does it make? I have to go."

She can't begin to say it. It can't be expressed, and even if it could, never could she give him such an advantage. It would be a forfeiture of power, and if not actual power, the appearance of possessing it. To say, My life, how I want it to look—it depends on you now. Without you, I can't have it. I know this.

In bed, she apologizes.

"It just seems like a big deal, Ted. I guess that's it. It would just seem like something you'd want to get off your chest."

"I know," he says.

"You two went to school together?"

"Yeah," he says.

"What did he do after?"

Her hand is on his sternum, which is as hard as wood.

"Oh," he says softly, letting out a breath. His eyes are closed. "Well, a little of everything. He was from Chicago, but he got his M.B.A. in California—he wasn't really sure what he wanted to do with it. He lived there for a long time, I think. He even lived here, I think. Before I moved here. The last I knew, he'd moved to Colorado. He had started to see someone seriously. I think they were engaged. He was—now *he* was an athlete."

Ted envies him. That much is certain. Still, he won't say much more, and though she won't admit it, Beth is relieved. To reveal more of Tom's life would be devastating, would be to recount adventures whose only purpose for Ted would be to make clear he'll never enjoy them again.

Beth knew Tom Mahoney, or at least boys like him. Mahoney was

the man everyone wanted to have at parties, meet up with for a drink
to talk about sports, figure out their brackets. The loudest boy at the
game, banging the empty plastic seat in front of him. He was pretty,
too. And kind. The one you could go to if you really wanted to talk
about a poem you were assigned to read or the chapter from the phi-
losophy book that set you thinking, knowing he would never make
fun of you. He was the figure all the boys drafted behind, knew they
could never surpass, but at the same time were never resentful of this
fact. Though the charm of Mahoney, at least to her, diminished the
older one got. If he was alluring in college and a bit after, he was
impractical now, though still powerful, still in possession of a quality
hard come by.

In the morning, Ted is gone again before she wakes. No note on the
bed (not that there needs to be), no e-mail waiting for her when she
arrives at work (he could have, from his BlackBerry), no call that
day, while she prepares, along with others and in spite of the weekend, to bring a company public.

That afternoon, she calls a friend she met at her gym, an art stu-
dent named Cleo, and they make plans to go to a burlesque show
way out in Northeast, a black neighborhood the first cab they hail
won't take them to. Beth wears worn jeans and a T-shirt with a picture of an ampersand, a pink lace scarf.

There, at the bar, they have two Irish Car Bombs, followed by
Guinness, watch the show, where a woman dressed like a cat in a
leotard, which displays one light-colored nipple, dances on a pole to
Edith Piaf songs and makes meowing sounds. Later, Beth listens to
Cleo talk about an installation she's working on at the Hirshhorn
with stamps, back copies of the *Philatelic,* and envelopes. Cleo asks
Beth how things are with Ted, and Beth says they've never been bet-
ter. Cleo wants to know if they've started shopping for rings, and
Beth doesn't know what to say, and so she says that there was a
grandmother. She corrects herself—a *great*-grandmother.

"An heirloom. Really, too big, but it's been in the family forever."

The bartender puts on an awful band, so loud that one has to look at people's lips to know what they are saying, and Beth feels for her purse, indicates that she thinks her phone is ringing, and she goes to the ladies' room. She does call Ted, though he doesn't answer. Thinks of him with his friends at a bar, trying the way young men try to mourn: clumsily, not sure how, not sure what words to say—to the family, to one another. So they drink, of course. Maybe tell a story or two, but even that is awkward, artificial. They all know what went on. They all know the light Mahoney offered, and, most important, they know to keep it a secret.

When she comes back, Cleo is talking to a young man in corduroy pants and a jean jacket, sideburns so thick, it makes her itch.

"Oh, Beth, this is Howard."

"Hi, Beth the lawyer," he says, "I'm Howard, the guy who will be hitting on you tonight."

"Hi, Howard the guy who will be hitting on me tonight. What's your good line for doing that?"

Cleo looks at Beth as if she might give Howard a chance. A look that says, He's funny at least. Entertainment.

"I just used it," he says, smiling a smile too confident. "That was pretty much it."

"I'm afraid," Beth says, "that you're going to have to do better than that."

"What do *you* think?" Howard asks Cleo. "Any good?"

"Hmm. Maybe. Halfway there. But really, it might be for nothing, since Beth here is practically married."

She is happy to hear Cleo say this.

"Married? I don't see a ring," Howard says.

"It's invisible," Beth says.

"It's so big that it actually bends light coming off it, so you can't really see it," Cleo shouts, laughing.

Beth unties the scarf around her neck.

"That's too bad," Howard says.

"Well, let's say I wasn't married, Howard the Duck. Let's say I wasn't and your terrific opening line, the line you use on all the girls you hit on—let's say it worked. What would you do then?"

Cleo looks at Beth, surprised. She smiles.

"I would talk to you," he says.

"And then?"

"I would see if you wanted to go out with me sometime."

"And do what?"

"Uh, I don't know. Get a drink. See a band."

"And let's say we did all that. Now it's time to go home—what would you do then?"

"Uh, I would take you home?"

"And what else?"

"What do you mean 'what else'?"

"Really, Howard, this is not going to work. You have to suggest something. Propose to *do* something. For once in your life. This sideburns and irony thing is not going to cut it, if we're to work out."

"Okay," Cleo says. "I think that's quite enough, young lady."

Beth touches Cleo on the arm.

"No. Howard here has got big plans for us. He's got a good alternative to me being married, which he thinks is a shame, and so I want to know my options here. What I've got to work with," Beth says to Cleo. "Howard," she says, setting her hands on his knees, "would you ask to come up to my place after our outstanding and revelatory date?"

"I might."

"And then you'd try to hold my hand and kiss me or something?"

"I would."

"And how would you do that?"

"Uh, I don't know."

"Mouth open or closed? Which?"

Howard is looking over Beth's shoulder. The burlesque dancer, who has come out from the back, is now wearing conservative black pants and a gray V-necked sweater, and Howard sees a way to escape, an excuse to talk to someone else.

"And then you'd want to—you know—fuck. Right, Howard? Or for me to fuck you? And then we'd hang out and drink coffee and see shows at the 9:30 Club and do what? What else? Howard, are you there?"

"Pardon me," he says, and gets up—this tall, lanky, thin kid—and walks away.

"Because I think it sounds pretty terrific!" Beth yells. *"Call me if you want to have a great life together, Howard! I'm ready when you are!"*

Deep night, no word from him, she goes through his things. Hidden in the corner of a closet there is a Johnnie Walker Black cardboard box in which he has stored items from law school, college, high school, boyhood.

There is a thin black folding Buck knife, a flask—a gift from one of his friend's weddings where he was a groomsman—with his initials, E.J.A., stenciled into the broadside. A class ring she's never seen. A Colibri lighter and cigar cutter. There is a digital watch that no longer keeps time. A magnifying glass, a set of keys. A whittled dog-eared copy of *Leaves of Grass*. Several books by Faulkner, all heavily annotated: *The Sound and the Fury, Light in August, Absalom, Absalom!* Was this a class he took? She picks up this last one and flips through, until she comes to a letter.

A plain white envelope, near the back of the book, sealed in flat like a leaf. She removes the envelope and slips out the letter inside. It is addressed to Ted Allison, an address in New York, from before he moved to Washington. The handwriting is in blue ink, written like a third grader:

Dear Ted Allison Randall Pink Floyd—

Hey, buddy—greetings from Colorado! I'm three days here and have set up camp (had to apply for a special permit) next to this little stream, a tributary of the Gunnison. I've included some pictures that I think say all that I would need to. I really wish that you were here. You would love it! I mean, absolutely.

*What's going on with you? How is Cathy Cotillion? Has she
given you an ultimatum yet? You may know this, but Sumner
said he heard that Darcy married some prof. in Las Cruces. Don't
feel bad.*

*I spoke with Brian and he's going to try to make it next year,
and so is Will, Robbie, my buddy Blake, and maybe even that guy
you met, Cody, so it would be good if you could, too. This time,
we split it—you're not paying for me. You really need to stop it
with that. What I did, I did because we're friends, Ted. That's
all. Case closed. Anyhow, it all just reminds me how much I miss
everyone, but I know we can work something out.*

*They were all upset to hear about Kristin, and maybe they
should be! I'm not saying it was easy. I don't need to explain to you
what it feels like.*

*Well, when you come to your senses and leave your job, we can
hook up somewhere. I know things are hard for you now, but I
think that it's just part of it. It'll work itself out. I hope that you
believe it, Ted. Well, that sounds like crap, I know, but I'm feeling
philosophical. If worse comes to worst, when I get back, we can go
abroad for a bit.*

Tom

P.S.: "Why do you hate the South?"

The letter is only seven years old and she does not know the
women mentioned: Cathy Cotillion (Oh God, what name did they
have for her?), Darcy. She knew a few of Ted's old girlfriends, but
that was more recent, since he'd been in Washington.

But what this Mahoney is talking about, Beth has no idea, and
she is worried. Alarmed, really. For what does Ted owe Tom? What
things are hard for him now? At the time, he would have been in
roughly the same place he is now—working. That was it. Younger
and greener, having had some difficulty acclimating to litigation,
but every attorney does. She did; everyone does.

She thinks of him with another girl, a Cathy or a Darcy, and thinks of his body, his shoulders, his calves with the one vein up the interior, thinks of him making love to these girls, having sex with these girls, his dick and how it looks inside another girl, and she becomes so angry that she tears up the letter from Tom Mahoney.

She's thirty-five. Seven years of schooling and she worked hard. There were fourteen weddings, at which she'd been a bridesmaid nine times, four times maid of honor. There had been eight baby namings that she had gone to, even one that Ted was invited to with her, but he didn't go.

It took a kind of rigor, but from the beginning she measured: She was Catholic; he was Presbyterian, though he didn't identify in any meaningful way. He was five eleven and she was five nine. He was fit like a marathoner. Drank but didn't smoke. Made a fantastic living, but it wasn't his life; he wasn't driven by it. Work took up too much of everyone's time. He wasn't especially political, and neither was she. A good lover—it wouldn't be a problem, and was it really the most important thing? Her friends liked him, always wanted to know where he was. *Where's old Teddy?* they'd say. *Give him a call and get his ass out here.* Even her sister admired him, the time she came to Washington to visit. Perhaps even a bit jealous. The room was better when Teddy was around. You could see it.

That Sunday morning she wakes and he is standing above her, wearing a black leather coat, a gray wool sweater, dark blue jeans, fine black leather shoes near her face. He is holding the scraps of dead Tom Mahoney's letter. In this light, he seems clearer, more defined than usual, brought into a greater relief.

"Oh. Oh God. I'm sorry, Ted," she says, crying. "I'm so, so sorry."

"You did this," he says.

She stands up. She tries to kiss him. Her breath is awful. He steps back. His small travel bag is near the threshold of the door.

"Where are the pictures?" he asks quickly. "What did you do with them?"

"They weren't there," she says, desperate, looking at the box, the books, his things, this great arsenal. "I promise. They weren't there. Please," she says.

He leans over, picking through the box. Then he stops, looks up, squints, for he has remembered where the photographs are, and is relieved. He stands up. He is again at ease, his body returned to its position of unending repose.

"Please," she says. "I'm so sorry. Just—please. Anything. I just—"

She thinks that he could hit her. That is the most obvious. It's happened to her before, though only once. Or he could just leave. Or ask that she leave. In this desperate moment, any might be okay. Bad, yes, awful, yes, but she has done something terrible, unforgivable. He is a sweet guy and what she did—she bullied him. Brutalized, in a way. Ted is at the very least nearly everything she might have wanted, though really, he is much more. Quite a bit more, to be sure. This is about what her future is worth to her, knowing that it's worth a great deal.

"Please tell me what you want me to do," she says, crying. "Tell me."

She looks at the pieces of this letter in his hand. Half a dozen are still on the floor. One segment with the word *Cotillion*. One with *ultimatum*. Another: *I miss everyone.*

She says it again: "Tell me." But he doesn't. He doesn't say anything. "Tell me what you want, Ted. Just say it. Name it."

He won't. What he does do, though, is that he brings her into him. She goes. An absolution she cannot believe. He wraps his arms around her. She puts her head into his chest and tries to say something to him—that she loves him, that she understands, that she doesn't *need* to understand, that she realizes that he has limits—everyone does—though it barely comes out, because he's holding her so close against his sweater, she cannot speak.

Later, running, she regards his body: White T-shirt soaked down to the small of his back, pressed against his skin. The muscle beneath shifting like plates. Arms full of blood, veins bloated like a farmer's. Calves divided discretely in half, quivering as each foot comes down. Remarkable. If she never knew anything else, she knew this quite well. Better than anyone. She really didn't need to know everything. Jogging behind him on a warm Halloween afternoon, the children trick-or-treating at the embassies on Massachusetts Avenue, slowing only for the one dear boy in a superhero costume who has turned around to watch them.

ACKNOWLEDGMENTS

I am grateful to Jill Kneerim for showing the first enthusiasm for this book. Her patience and guidance, as well as that of Caroline Zimmerman, brought these pages so far along. Also, I am grateful to George Witte, my editor, for understanding Tom Mahoney in the same way I do.

Some of these stories appeared previously in literary journals, and I'd like to acknowledge those editors: Evelyn Somers, Speer Morgan, Brock Clarke, Nicola Mason, Celia Johnson, Tricia Callahan, Maria Gagliano, John Irwin, and Abe Greenwald. I would particularly like to acknowledge Cara Blue Adams and the late Jeanne Leiby at *The Southern Review.*

I've been very lucky to work with writers who have encouraged me early on and who continue to provide advice and support—my teachers, friends, and classmates in the Writing Seminars at Johns Hopkins University, and, when I was just starting out, Fred Shafer and Jeff White.

Several friends read early drafts of these stories, providing feedback, and I'd like to thank them: Adam Heltzer, Chris Castro, Lee Woocher, Peter Coco, Darcelle Bleau, Tim O'Keefe, Traci O'Dea, and Daniel Heltzer.

For the tremendous belief and encouragement of my family and my wife, Shari, I owe much.